PUFFIN CANADA

ONE FOR SORROW

MARY C. SHEPPARD was born in Corner Brook,
Newfoundland, and has spent more than twenty-
five years working in the media. Mary has a B.A.
from St. Francis Xavier University and an M.Sc. in
journalism from Columbia University. Mary is the
executive producer of CBCNews.ca and lives with
her family in Toronto.

She visits her sisters in Newfoundland regularly.
Her first novel, *Seven for a Secret*, won the Ruth
Schwartz Award (now called the Ruth and Sylvia
Schwartz Award) in 2002.

Also by Mary C. Sheppard

Seven for a Secret

ONE FOR SORROW MARY C. SHEPPARD

Tales from Cook's Cove

PUFFIN
CANADA

PUFFIN CANADA

Published by the Penguin Group

Penguin Group (Canada), 90 Eglinton Avenue East, Suite 700, Toronto, Ontario, Canada M4P 2Y3
(a division of Pearson Canada Inc.)

Penguin Group (USA) Inc., 375 Hudson Street, New York, New York 10014, U.S.A.
Penguin Books Ltd, 80 Strand, London WC2R 0RL, England
Penguin Ireland, 25 St Stephen's Green, Dublin 2, Ireland (a division of Penguin Books Ltd)
Penguin Group (Australia), 250 Camberwell Road, Camberwell, Victoria 3124, Australia
(a division of Pearson Australia Group Pty Ltd)
Penguin Books India Pvt Ltd, 11 Community Centre, Panchsheel Park, New Delhi – 110 017, India
Penguin Group (NZ), 67 Apollo Drive, Rosedale, North Shore 0632, New Zealand (a division of
Pearson New Zealand Ltd)
Penguin Books (South Africa) (Pty) Ltd, 24 Sturdee Avenue, Rosebank, Johannesburg 2196,
South Africa

Penguin Books Ltd, Registered Offices: 80 Strand, London WC2R 0RL, England

First published 2008

1 2 3 4 5 6 7 8 9 10 (WEB)

Copyright © Mary C. Sheppard, 2008

Definitions excerpted from the *Dictionary of Newfoundland English*, second edition, edited by
G.M. Story, W.J. Kirwin and J.D.A. Widdowson (1990). Reproduced with kind permission from
University of Toronto Press.

Manufactured in Canada.

ISBN-10: 0-14-305413-9
ISBN-13: 978-0-14-305413-9

LIBRARY AND ARCHIVES CANADA CATALOGUING IN PUBLICATION

Sheppard, Mary C. (Mary Catherine), 1952–
One for sorrow / Mary C. Sheppard.

ISBN 978-0-14-305413-9

I. Title.

PS8587.H385345O54 2008   jC813'.6   C2007-905784-5

Visit the Penguin Group (Canada) website at **www.penguin.ca**

Special and corporate bulk purchase rates available; please see
www.penguin.ca/corporatesales or call 1-800-810-3104, ext. 477 or 474

For my sisters: Anita, Norma, Linda, Loretta, Lorraine, Jackie, and Honorah; and my brother, George.

ONE FOR SORROW

Newfoundland

Area of detail

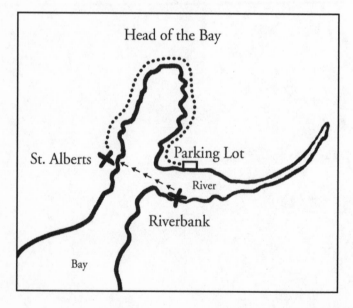

Head of the Bay

St. Alberts

Parking Lot

River

Riverbank

Bay

•••••••• road around the Bay to St. Alberts

← ← ← ← skating across the ice

One for sorrow
Two for joy
Three for a wedding
Four for a boy
Five for silver
Six for gold
Seven for a secret that can't be told.

CHAPTER ONE

Best kind: indicating general approval

Folks say that out of bad often comes good. It took me a long time to see the good in anything the long, cold winter my beloved great-aunt died.

You see, I had a pretty miserable life growing up in Riverbank. I was the baby who broke my mother's health and ruined my older sister's life. Louise had good reason to despise the sight of me from the day I was born.

"I can't believe I came home for someone as stupid as Issy," Louise said whenever she got really mad over the years, not caring whether or not I heard. I saw the resentment in my sister's eyes every time they darted around a room looking to blame someone, mostly me, for her sad life.

Louise got an emergency call some fifteen years ago when she was starting a summer job in St. John's, after finishing her first year at Memorial University. She was told over the phone that Mother had taken ill with stomach pains and was being rushed to hospital in Grand Falls, which was across the narrow river and up a hundred-mile gravel road from our home. Louise rode the bus for five hours from the opposite direction and got to the hospital in time to be told that she had a tiny baby sister (that would be me). She had barely taken me in her arms when the nurses stampeded past her for what they were yelling was a Code Nine, and they were heading for my mother's room. Louise followed the commotion and that's how the two of us witnessed our mother dying and being jump-started back to life. Needless to say, I remember nothing of the nurses pounding my mother's chest, though I've been told the story so many times I can feel the drama of it in my very bones. The whole scene eventually made my most-likely-to-succeed sister into a sour schoolmarm and a prissy old maid. And me, well, at home I was like a sad dog, keeping my head down, tying not to be a magnet for trouble.

Louise left university and took the place of a mother in my everyday world. She told me once that Mother took one look at the child with the bad eye, turned her face to the wall and refused to have anything to do with me. Louise cared for Mother mostly without a fuss, but my sister and I have been at odds with each other just about all my life, except for the rare truce. Even as a baby I can vaguely remember her resentment toward me.

As good as Louise was to Mother, she could be spitey and mean with me. Maybe it was because I dressed like Elly May on *The Beverly Hillbillies* and she couldn't bear to have a hair out of place. Or maybe she was too young to take on so much responsibility. Or maybe it was because I was no good at school work, while she motored her way through a fat book every week. People like her had no time or patience for dumb people like me. I liked the outdoors more than being cooped up in the house. I preferred to paint a fence rather than decorate dainty bookmarks with glossy flowers. I understood this, and I tried not to waste her time.

ONCE I GOT OUT of the house, I had it pretty good. I could be as shy as a ghost in daylight, but I found my little bits of happiness wherever I could. Walking with my dog, Bush, glued to my side was a great comfort. On dark and cold nights, I was welcome in many homes, especially if I brought along a plate of scones, a specialty our English mother had taught me and Louise to make, or some gingersnaps from an old family recipe handed down by our great-aunt Lady. A hot cup of tea would appear and I was happy to sit back in a corner and watch TV with a family not my own. Neither the adults nor the little ones cared about my eye and me not being able to get beyond grade nine.

I especially liked to visit Mildred Spence. She was only fourteen, but she had more or less quit school. She had not been a full week at school since she was ten. She had six younger brothers and sisters, and it was she who got them all out the door every day, made their lunches and had a hot meal on the table when they got home. After supper she cleaned off the kitchen table and made sure each one of them did every scrap of homework. Mildred never once whined about her lot in life. Her mother lay in bed most days, staring at the walls, smoking pack after pack of Player's cigarettes, and her dad had a bad back and could work only a few months each year.

Her home could have been like mine, but it wasn't, because Mildred happily looked after her family. She would often say that she was no good at school work herself and that it was her calling to look after people. Her one wish was that all her sisters and brothers would graduate high school. Bush and I would sit with Mildred's mom, who loved rubbing Bush's big, furry back, while Mildred got on with her chores.

My dear great-aunt Lady always had a warm spot saved for me beside her old wood stove, and Mrs. John, the blind old woman up around the bend, well, her round wrinkled face practically shone like the moon on a velvet night when she heard my footsteps. I'd help her sort her wools into a different basket for each colour so she could crochet beautiful cushions from patterns her hands knew from memory.

And the little ones at school, they wouldn't leave me alone. They tugged at my sweaters, clung to my coat and looked up at me with trusting eyes. I was the one who took their side in a school-yard full of bullies. I'd take them up the river for summer picnics and to gather berries, or to fish with little poles I stripped from the trees. The children loved Bush and he loved them all right back. And Bush reminded me of the time when I had a cherished, true friend all my own, and that too helped me cope.

I didn't run with the teen crowd, but I didn't hold that against anyone. The truth was, I couldn't bear to let anyone see how stupid I was. I could hide it from Lady, from an old blind woman and poor Mildred, from the kiddies and even my dog, but no way could I hide it from the crowd I went to school with. They knew and they pitied me, and I couldn't stand pity. So it was me who turned away from them—until they wouldn't let me anymore.

ONE THING I LEARNED early is that it's not so easy to come back to life. My mother continued to keep to her bed most days, recovering from the heart attack that had almost killed her two hours after I was born. She spent some of her time lounging on the chesterfield, drinking tea and eating chocolates and biscuits, getting fatter and fatter and bossing us around. I'd heard the gossip: "Her heart is just fine, but Agnes never got over having a baby eighteen years after being told she could never have another child." The neighbours seldom noticed that I was in the room, listening to every word. I had come as an extra enormous shock to my mother, because with her being a rather large, sickly woman at the time, she didn't know she was pregnant until the doctor admitted her to the maternity ward at the hospital.

Mother made sure we knew her life was wretched. Definitely not the suffering-in-silence type. Deep in my heart I believed she had given up wanting to get better. If she did, she would lose her companion and maid, my sister, who handled Mother like she was a fragile egg.

Before she became a doormat, my sister had a real life. I'd heard a thousand times that she'd been an amazing student and was planning to become a university professor and teach about books, something of which there seemed to be an endless supply, because she was always reading one. Mrs. John had even hinted there was a handsome boy with a broken heart in her past. Sometimes I felt sorry for my sister, but most of the time I didn't. Most of the time I thought it was her own fault. There had to be at least a dozen ways to leave a bad life. Cars left the parking lot on the other side of the river every month loaded with people heading to Ontario to find jobs. It couldn't be that hard to get back on the bus that had brought her home. And as the old 1966 song "Come Home to Newfoundland" went, Air Canada lands here every day and there are ferries to take you across the bay. This was equally good advice for getting off the island. Even simple me had a plan, for goodness' sake.

Up until she died, Lady had been the main reason my life wasn't a total wreck. Often when I was growing up, I would go to her house after school and just sit and watch her working at her rolltop desk in the corner of her living room, or parlour, as she still liked to call it. The room now boasted a small colour television, given to her by my father, and a telephone with one of the first private lines in Riverbank. Or I'd hold skeins of wool, careful to extend my arms out straight, so she could loop the yarn into a ball. She loved to knit, and I loved to sit and watch the wool go through her needles as a long string of colour and then appear again as a leaf or a star on the front of a sweater or the edge of a scarf. The click-clack of her needles soothed me, because when she was knitting, she expected nothing from me; it was enough to know that I was there, keeping out of trouble.

By the time I was ten, I was the one who got her tea and her supper, because by then her arthritic hands could no longer hold the heavy kettle or lift the dampers on her cast-iron stove. I learned how to make the lacy oat cookies and the gingersnaps she used to have waiting for me after school. I kept her stove going by piling in the wood chunks before school and leaving bits of wood just the right size for her hands. Dad, on one of his trips home, devised a special cover for her stove that meant she could just drop in the wood without having to lift a damper. Each evening I banked the fire again to get her through the night. Sometimes, if she had a cold or trouble breathing from her asthma, I'd stay the night and make her tea when the coughing got too bad.

Everyone, including me, called my great-aunt Lady. She was my father's father's sister, and from the moment I could toddle across the lane to her big wide veranda and her old-fashioned pantry with its glass cookie jar, I took to her. She was the grandmother I never had, because my father's mother died from the complications of childbirth a week after he was born.

I can hear you asking where my father was while I was being born. I had the misfortune of coming into the world in June, while Dad was on one of his long trips. He was a third engineer on the coastal steamers at the time, and he worked along the south shore with special trips up north. That time he was in Labrador, trapped in a late ice storm. By the time he got to Grand Falls, my mother was breathing on her own again and I had attached myself to Louise. He too was stunned at having another child, as well as a wife at death's door who would never recover from the blow. Louise said he took it all in and signed up for the ferries crossing between Port aux Basques and North Sydney. Better money for sure, with a promotion to second engineer, and the added bonus of longer stints away from home.

Being a very practical and matter-of-fact person, Louise knew she couldn't abandon our mother or me. There was a leash around her neck that got tighter and tighter as months dripped into years. By the time I was fifteen, my sister could no more leave my mother than a lobster could claw its way out of a trap. Part of me wanted to see her break away, but in the depths of my soul I knew she couldn't jump in a car or get on a bus and that a plane was beyond comprehension. She was shackled to Mother's bedpost with the ties that bind. Still, I resented her for making it seem like it was mostly my fault that she couldn't get on with her life. In fact, it was her own fault for letting Mother depend on her so much.

I heard a few times too often about how miserable it was that she'd never been able to get back to St. John's to clean out her room in the boarding house. I was three weeks premature, a weak, cranky baby who didn't feed well, and she walked the floor with me day and night for months. Louise said I was as scrawny and pitiful as the lone starving crow she swore she saw out the hospital window when the nurses handed me to her. She liked teasing me by saying she knew then that I was headed for one sorrowful life.

THE THINGS THAT LOUISE HAD to leave behind in the boarding house had eventually arrived back home in boxes tied up with nylon fishing twine. By the time I was five or six, the boxes had been pushed to a dark corner of the shed out back. I got into them one summer and played dress-up by wearing Louise's twin-sets and flared skirts of the mid-1950s.

Louise was pretty enough a long time ago. I remember her wearing soft sweaters and wanting to be with her, wanting to see her smile, wanting to touch her long, golden-red hair. There's a large graduation photo of her with dimples and bright eyes and a wide smile, the smart kid going places. But that's not the Louise I had to deal with the winter before I turned sixteen. We had drifted apart long ago. She had turned into someone the cat wouldn't bring home, all tight lips, furrowed brow, and accusing eyes, her golden curls stretched back into a braid that did not frame her narrow face well at all (couldn't she see this?). She was tall and walked with a stoop, arms often pressed against her flat chest, unfriendly and closed.

Her clothes were dismal. She no longer wore any pretty things. Her high school prom dress that she stored in a plastic bag and modelled for me once when I was about eight had disappeared entirely. She had looked like a fairy in the layers and layers of silver net and shiny satin. I was not a good dresser either; Louise ordered what I needed from the catalogues without ever noticing what was in style. Yet it was 1970, for goodness' sake; the minis and maxis had passed her by, and so did net stockings, bell-bottoms, gold-rimmed glasses and halter tops. She was up there in front of the classroom day after day, and you'd have thought she'd give her little pupils something to look at besides her knee-length black skirt and navy long-sleeved blouse on Monday, Wednesday and Friday, and her navy skirt and black turtleneck sweater on Tuesday and Thursday. With her hair pulled back, her pinched lips and the black cat's-eye glasses she'd got five years earlier, she was but a washed-out shadow of the young girl I vaguely remember. She looked every inch the small-town-and-very-serious school principal that she was.

It was the way she stuck to rules and routines that really bothered me. In the morning, up at seven on the dot, breakfast at eight, exactly; at night, homework from seven to nine, even though I hardly ever understood a word of it. But I learned to put up with her drill-sergeant ways. By keeping things organized, she was able to work full time and look after Mother full time.

What she didn't know was that my secret plan did not include hanging around the house to wait on Mother. No way. I felt no guilt about it. Louise could continue to manage everything. She was that kind of person, and I was not. School was going nowhere for me, and I knew that lots of girls from our place didn't graduate high school but still managed to find jobs in Toronto. Some were even going out to Alberta, to Fort McMurray. Though people here knew me as being shyer than a pine martin, I was working on getting up my nerve to quit school and leave this place as soon as I turned sixteen, on Midsummer's Day. Lady used to give me a bit of a hard time when I'd talk about not finishing high school. Sometimes she'd warn me about the big world out there, where you needed a good education. Sometimes she'd remind me that I couldn't run away from my troubles, and sometimes she'd tell me that I could succeed if I would just let my family help me. I'd want to toss my head when Lady said this last one, but I knew she loved me and tears would well in my eyes at the thought of letting her down.

When I was with Lady or visiting in Riverbank, I was calm and happy. But I got angry and annoyed the moment I walked through the door of our house. Maybe it was the smell of the Evergreen spray that Louise used to keep Mother's room smelling fresh that clung to our clothes, or maybe it was my mother's whines that triggered my upsets.

I loved the silent river that gently separated our quiet place from the ruckus of the mainland, the pretty, soft hills barely

covered by thin, wispy grass or blown snow, the miles of beckon-
ing rocky barrens, the shallow ponds, the jellybean-coloured
houses, the freedom to come and go as I pleased, the sense that I
belonged. But the winter after Lady died, while it almost broke my
heart, I decided that I had to make a choice about the rest of my
life before I got tangled up for good in the net of misery and woe
that was my family.

As it turned out, after "the accident" I wasn't so sure anymore
about anything.

LADY, THE PERSON I loved most in the world, left me all her
money, five hundred dollars, enough to get me to the mainland
and get myself settled. I didn't know anything about school work,
but I knew about money and the doors it could open. Before I had
the money I knew exactly what I wanted to do—quit school and
work in the kitchen of a fishing and hunting camp up the river—
but the money made me realize I could move far away. And far was
good. Louise went into a tizzy whenever she saw me counting the
twenty-dollar bills and humming "Happy Birthday," reminding
her that the day I turned sixteen I could leave without the police
chasing after me.

"You'd better smarten up if you think you can live off five
hundred dollars. It won't last a month in a big city. It's your turn
to look after Mother. I'm the one who should be leaving, not you."

I would drive her crazy with the smirk on my face when she
said that, and then I'd do a sprint to the bathroom and lock the
door real quick to get away from her. We both knew there wasn't
any way I could manage Mother, and that Mother couldn't stand

me and my sulks and my backwardness. Anyway, Louise had been saying the same thing for all of my fifteen years and she was still here. Now, though, when she said it, my sister's mouth got tighter and she seemed to be on the verge of a scream or howl.

It was two weeks after Lady's funeral when Louise announced one evening after supper that something had to change around here. "It was never my idea to come home, kiddo. It's your fault I'm still here," she said as she tucked a thick wool blanket around Mother. "That child ruined my life," she told Mother, "and it's finally time I took care of myself. I'm going to teach her to read every one of your medicine bottles this winter. I don't care how many hours it takes. I won't be the one stuck here until I die just because she refuses to learn."

Mother gasped with astonishment, the water glass for her pills stopped halfway to her lips. But she found her voice as fast as a babbling brook. "You can't go anywhere as long as I need you here, and that's that. How am I supposed to manage on my own? That child is a moron and a hellcat. Don't be silly, Louise. Where do you think you might go, anyway? No decent girl leaves her mother until she marries. Besides, you've already wasted too much time trying to help her with her studying. She's too dumb for words, and that's just the way it is. Hand me my knitting."

This was the fine answer from a mother with a heart as cold as a granite headstone. Mother didn't notice how fierce Louise looked. In all my life I had never heard her threaten to leave with such determination.

I couldn't help but feel smug when Mother scolded Louise. But I had the sense not to let Louise see me. She would find out soon enough that being an angel of mercy was a life sentence. She wasn't going anywhere. Not a chance, no way!

That particular day I remember sneaking back to my room, turning on my small transistor radio and humming along with the Beatles while thinking about what Louise had said about teaching me to read. Was it possible, I wondered, after so many years of trying?

At fifteen, I was tired of being a big stupid girl in grade nine, which I was doing for the second time after being pushed through all the other grades. I wanted to read, and I was ready to try with every bone in my body. But I had to be careful, too. If I learned, I asked myself, would that mean being lured into my mother's spiderweb, being sucked into her sphere of helplessness?

MY GREAT-AUNT'S REAL NAME was Ladysmith, after a place in Africa where her father had some luck in a gold rush before establishing himself as a merchant in Newfoundland. But she came to be known as Lady, and no one could ever tell me if she became like a lady because that was her name. She had a gentle kindness and the knack of always knowing the right thing to say. She had a little plaque on the wall as you came in her front door that spelled out her code of honour: *There's so much good in the worst of us; and so much bad in the best of us; that it ill behoves any of us to talk about the rest of us.* She was the best kind. I felt safe in her home—me and Bush together. Lady genuinely liked my chocolate brown Labrador, unlike Mother, who often said that animals, especially big dogs, should never be allowed inside a house.

If Lady was leaning with a strained back over her accounting work, I would sit quietly and wait, and soon enough she would snap down the top of her desk, smooth out her dress and ask me to bring in a tray of tea and dainty macaroons, a delicacy she had taught me to make crispy on the outside and chewy on the inside. Sometimes at night we would toast homemade bread on a twisted coat hanger over her ancient stove. She did not expect me to talk about silly things. She would tell me stories of when she lived in London during and after the Great War. She'd talk mostly about her walks through the beautiful parks, her little house that backed onto the River Thames and how much she enjoyed working for the government.

Starting when I was very young, she, the trained bookkeeper, would ask me to add up numbers. Later she and I did the multiplication tables together, and then she took to giving me long strings of numbers to add and subtract in my head.

I got to be very good at math. But that was the only subject I passed. I could not read, and unless some miracle happened very soon, I was never going to read. So it was time for me to accept my fate in life, quit school and get out of Riverbank. Then my sister, who had this idea that we were a family to be looked up to (you know the kind of thing—she was the principal, Dad was an engineer, Lady had lived in London and was the daughter of a fish merchant, and Mother was from England and had her nose in the air about being better than all the people in Riverbank), could forget she had a sister who wasn't up to scratch.

The wind was blowing the soft snow over the crest of the hill on the early November day when we buried Lady. I shivered in the black Sunday coat that let the cold creep into my back and chest as I said goodbye to my best friend. My father, a mostly silent man, saw how much I suffered. He put his arm around my hunched shoulders and whispered, "There, there, her time had come." Empty words for a broken heart.

Lady had kept me tethered to our place, and on the day we put her in the ground I knew it was time. I promised on her grave that I would leave the house I called home the day I legally could.

MY WHOLE FAMILY was contrary at the beginning of that winter, more so than was normal even for us. Louise was on my back about homework all through November and into December. She was determined I was going to read come hell or high water. I'd want to look out the window to see if the river was frozen, and if she saw my gaze so much as drift in that direction she'd get up and close the curtains with a sharp little snap of her skinny hand. Mother asked for cups of tea at all hours and was picky with Louise about spoons that weren't quite polished enough, linen napkins that weren't ironed into precise creases and bacon that should have been crisper and hotter.

It was especially hard because in the past, when Louise got mean or Mother went on one of her tirades, Lady had been my refuge. Now I looked across the lane and saw her house boarded up for the winter, until Dad could get home to deal with it. He had gone through the house when he was home for the funeral and left it pretty much the way it was the day Lady died in her sleep. "One of my girls might want to make her nest there soon," he said with a wink toward Louise. He was dreaming in Technicolor. The old house would probably rot away because no young people today wanted a home that would always look weathered and fragile, with no heating or electricity upstairs and a kitchen that still had the wood stove Lady bought in 1952. They wanted bungalows now, with picture windows and dishwashers. Lady's bright, homey cushions were still on her chesterfield and her bits of china remained in her kitchen cupboard, though Louise and I each took a pretty china cup and saucer painted with yellow roses as a keepsake.

Just before Christmas, Louise came up with the idea of putting words on flash cards for me, but the brainstorm was a total failure. Whatever card she held up in the air, the squiggles all looked the same to me. It was the old problem I'd had for as long as I could remember. Sometimes, if the letters were really big or if I twisted my head at a certain angle, I could see them. But Louise hated it when I jerked my shoulders and squinted my eyes; she said I looked like a real moron. Louise had a calm, soothing voice when she was teaching, but words like "imbecile," "stupid," "retarded," "birdbrain" and "numbskull" sounded bad no matter what tone she used.

Times like that, I would reach for Bush and knead his thick brown fur along his solid back. I would think about Mrs. John, who treasured each of my visits, and of the children who looked up to me with trust and open hearts. Sometimes I'd even go back a few years and remember my friend Wish, a boy who talked to me like I was as normal as any of his other friends.

Looking back, I have to wonder if the accident was waiting to happen. People often say that, and in our case it might just be true.

Surely something had to change. Surely we two sisters couldn't hate each other to our graves.

THE SCHOOL WAS FILLED with the giggles of small children that day. The little ones spent recess taping their paper Christmas stockings along the main hallway. I helped them when their arms wouldn't stretch to the hanging rail. I saw my sister out of the corner of my eye supervising her grade three students with her usual grimness, but since we always ignored each other anyway in the school, I ignored her that day too. After hanging the stockings, each of the lower grades went back to their classrooms to get ready for a little party later in the day, where they could gorge themselves on hard Christmas candy, nuts, potato chips, cookies and soda pop.

So I was very surprised when, an hour later, my teacher called me out of our classroom and told me that my sister needed me. I never got called out of the classroom; all the teachers had given up on me and let me be, and my sister never ever needed me.

The grade three classroom was only two doors away, and I was there in an instant. The children were as quiet as mice eating stolen cheese, sitting at their desks, eyes frozen to one spot—my sister on her knees cradling a child's head in her lap.

The child was Rosalie Peterson, one of the kids the others always picked on. She wore eyeglasses, her nose was always snotty and she never had a tissue. Her skin was pale and her blue eyes were almost too big for her solemn little round face. She was hesitant and unsure about everything. From her first day at school she had been left out of whatever was going on unless her mother or sister interfered. From time to time Mrs. Peterson would insist that Rosalie get invited to a birthday party, or Rosalie would come to school with a box of chocolates for the class and the children would like her for the length of time it took to eat them.

It was odd that they all got away with treating her like a leper. She was, after all, a Peterson. The Petersons were the family my mother wanted us to be. They owned the one general store in Riverbank and they also owned one of the camps upcountry for rich Americans to fly-fish salmon in the summer and shoot moose in the fall. Rosalie's sister, Beryl, the one in my grade that year, had at least a dozen miniskirts and half a dozen pairs of amazingly high platform heels from the stores in St. John's. (I didn't care about the skirts and heels, but I loved her navy pea jacket with brass buttons and secretly wanted one just like it.) Mrs. Peterson prepared the priest's roast beef dinner after Mass on the Sundays he could make it across the river to our little church.

I took to Rosalie from the day she started school. She was a sweet child who was bursting to be liked. Most days, I sat on a bench in the children's playground and dared any of the mean kids to touch her.

"She asked for you just before she fainted the second time," said Louise, explaining why she had sent for me. "Miss Simms is calling the new doctor to see what he wants us to do," she continued as Rosalie came round, saw me and reached for my hand.

"Does your head hurt, my dear?" asked my sister in the gentlest voice I ever heard come out of her mouth. Rosalie moaned and her eyes rolled up inside her head. This looked very frightening, and my heart froze.

"Get the other children out of here," Louise whispered as she laid Rosalie out flat on the floor. I jumped up and saw the fear in her classmates' eyes. I forced a smile and pointed toward the door; the children went instantly. I was about to send them outside, but a quick glance out the window showed that the morning sunshine had disappeared and a raw wind had picked up. I directed them to the small school library instead.

The last child was leaving his desk when Miss Simms came rushing to the door. "The doctor says we have to get her to the hospital. He says he doesn't like the sound of it. I can't get hold of the Petersons. Beryl is home sick with the flu and she says her parents went to Grand Falls for the day." With that, she looked at Louise and me and reached for the doorjamb to support herself.

Louise sat back on her heels. "Rosalie's heart is racing, her skin is cool. We'll need blankets and a sleigh. Issy, go home and get our skates, we have to take her across the river with not a minute to spare. Miss Simms, tell the doctor we'll need the ambulance waiting at the shore down near the Point. I think they'll be taking her right into Grand Falls."

I ran home as fast as a shooting star. I crashed into our back porch and grabbed my black hockey skates and Louise's old Barbara Ann Scott figure skates hanging on the nails there. No way would Rosalie wake again and not find me there beside her.

By the time I got back to the school, Rosalie was coming round. She was as white as marble but wrapped snugly in thick blankets and stretched out on a toboggan padded with cushions from the teachers' room. Louise and I laced up our skates and we each took the rope on the toboggan and headed down over the hill and onto the ice. A very anxious crowd waved and waved until we rounded the little forest near the shoreline. The ice was always a risk and there'd been open patches only yesterday. I'd seen them myself from the cemetery when I went for a walk up there to visit Lady. But we'd had a very cold night and that's what I tried to think about as we set out into the fierce and biting wind.

On the ice, without the trees to break its force, the northwest wind was brutal. We braced ourselves as we headed into snow squalls with our charge, skating in as straight a line as we could to where the ambulance was flashing its light. Because the wind kept pushing us off course, it took us much longer than usual to cross the river, but the red beacon gave us a goal.

The ice was thick in the part of the river approaching the Point, and when we finally got there and stumbled over the ice drifts near the shore, the doctor took Rosalie into his arms and laid her on the stretcher. He took out his stethoscope and listened to Rosalie's breathing, then nodded to the driver to get ready to go.

"You did the right thing to bring her over," said the doctor, who had only arrived in our parts a few weeks earlier. He rummaged through his black bag and jumped up into the back of the ambulance while the driver sputtered out of the deep snow. The last thing we saw through the window was the roly-poly doctor bracing himself against the back door as he filled a needle.

Once the stress of getting there and putting Rosalie into good hands was over, I started to shiver. There we were on the ice, two miles from home, cold to the bone, and thick, wet snow had begun to swirl around us. We had to go back right away; the last thing you wanted was to be on the ice in the dark, and the closest house on this side of the river was five miles up the road.

Another reason Louise often lost her patience with me was that I couldn't tell time on a watch or clock. Instead, I learned to tell it with shadows and light and the height of the sun in the sky. So, even before Louise said, "Oh my goodness, it's 3:45 and it'll be dark soon. We had better leave the tobaggan," I knew we would have to skate fast and hard.

The wind was at our back, and for a few minutes it was absolutely exhilarating. Down the middle of the river was all black, fresh ice. I spread my arms to skim the air like an eagle.

I saw the open water too late. What had been solid ice when we left was now slush, and we were headed right for it, going so fast there was no way to stop. I hit the water with a dull splash. Louise was but a second behind me.

As numb as I was, I turned toward my sister and let out a low gasp of horror. A trickle of blood was coming from her head, and then her head fell forward into the water. I reached out and grabbed her around the neck just as she was sliding under the shards of ice.

I remember thinking that if I stopped kicking for the both of us, there'd be no more not meeting expectations, no more scolding. There'd be just nothing. Maybe I'd even find Lady. And then I rallied. I knew I didn't want to die. I remembered that I'd jumped ice pans with my skates on for childish games and told myself I could darn well swim with them on, too. The shore wasn't far, just ten yards. The tricky part would be getting out of the water and onto the ice, which might give way under our weight. I was thinking hard and I was conscious of every second passing. Louise was ridiculously thin and, despite everything, I realized I was very afraid for her.

"Don't, Issy, you get ashore, leave me. Every second counts," she managed to say into my ear between gasping breaths.

I was frantic and kicked toward the shoreline. I expected her to blame me for the accident; I did not expect her to tell me to cut loose and forget about her. I got so mad I found the strength to keep our heads above water for another minute.

That's when I heard Bush barking and people shouting on the shore. "Hang on, hang on, don't let go, whatever you do, don't stop moving." I gathered all my strength, kicked more slowly and let my mind go blank.

"We've got a rope. We can see that Miss Heffernan is hurt. You have to get the rope around her first, Issy, you have to be strong."

I didn't know who was talking to me. People were easing their way toward us, stretched out flat on the ice. When one person was a body length away from the open water, he tossed me the rope. I put it around Louise with shaking, frozen hands. She was as white as a sand-washed seashell. I wasn't even sure if she was alive when I signalled them to pull. I counted the seconds, each one sending a million blasts of icy pain through my body. Fifteen seconds of eternity passed before it was my turn. My hands went stiff and I couldn't find the strength for one more kick. I felt my head slipping under the water and was thinking how lovely it would be to just drift away. It was so soothing. The water turned warm, as warm and lovely as a bath after a skin-piercing rain.

Almost at the same instant I felt a hot burning in my lungs. A hand and then a strong arm grabbed and pushed me back up into the air. I fought. I kicked and tried to bite the hand that was tugging at my ponytail. The air was so cold, my body hurt so much. But no one was listening to me. A rope went over my head, and like a baby harp seal I was pulled onto the ice.

Soon we were rolled into blankets and on hands and knees we were pulled gently toward other outstretched hands and arms, all ready to help in every way they could. Bush was all over me then, licking, jumping, thumping his tail. I heard Louise whimpering and then coughing up water—the most wonderful sounds I ever heard coming from her in my life.

I turned on my side, and in my confusion I thought I was dead and seeing a ghost. The third person on the ice, the one who must have jumped in to push me out, was also huddled in blankets, shivering and trying to get up. He was someone I felt I must know, but my brain was muddled. More precisely, he looked like someone I used to know, but that person had left me long ago, taking my young heart with him.

Then everything went black.

They rushed us toward the closest house along the beach. Someone was forcing dark Jamaican rum between my chattering teeth as I came to, the first that had ever passed my lips. Women's hands helped me into thick, dry clothes and wrapped me in more blankets heated on the back of a wood stove. Mrs. Blackwood, the woman who tended to many of our troubles when we couldn't get to the doctor, cleaned the deep cut on Louise's head and stitched it up with plain white thread and a needle that had been sterilized over a candle. Just as well that Louise fainted dead away.

CHAPTER TWO

Rhyme of oaths: a sustained string of oaths;
a fit of cursing

D r. McKay came over to Riverbank two days after Rosalie went to the hospital. He knocked at our door to thank us for saving the child's life and to tell us she would be fine now that it was known she had diabetes. He said that most people come out of diabetic shock by eating food but that it was tricky in Rosalie's case because she had never been diagnosed with low-sugar problems. He said none of us could have known what to do for her and that our speed in getting her to the ambulance saved her life.

I was lying on the couch in the living room when the doctor came to call. My chest still hurt—not from the cold, but from the fight to bring me to the surface.

"You should be in the hospital yourself, young lady," he said as he took my temperature and listened to my lungs. "These are nasty bruises, one rib is cracked, and you need to rest," he said as he reached for a box of pills in his black bag and told me he would be back the next day.

Over the next few months we learned a lot about Dr. McKay. He was forty-five years old and first came to Newfoundland from England as a boy. His father had been stationed in St. John's with the British navy for a few years during the war. This intrigued my mother. She kept trying to recall if she had met his mother when she was in St. John's during the same years.

"Do you think your parents knew the Perry family?" she would ask. Or, "Did your mother ever tell you if she went to the Regatta Ball?"

He went back to England with his parents after the war, but the island clung to him. He said he could never see a rock or smell a fog without feeling Newfoundland in his bones. Then one day he saw an advertisement placed by the Newfoundland government for doctors to work in isolated clinics. He came to our bay with a coastline covering a hundred miles of coves and inlets and several thousand people, most of whom only ever saw a doctor when they took it into their heads to drive the two hours up the gravel highway to Grand Falls, or another hour on to Gander, where there was a military base, the international airport and a bigger hospital.

Dr. David, as he soon asked us to call him, wasn't a tall man. He was a bit porky, really. How else can I describe a man who had a thick waistline, wobbly cheeks and a flabby neck? He was losing hair from the top of his head and what was left was spread about in little thatches. He wore steel-rimmed square glasses that looked like they were issued from the bottom of the barrel by a government office. If you picked at him, you could see these things. Altogether, though, he was presentable enough—not handsome or anything, but you could get used to him and his round belly. Everyone adored his English accent, and people stopped to talk to him just to hear him say "righty-oh," or "jumper" when he clearly meant "sweater," or "tea" when it was time for supper.

The most annoying thing about him was that he never looked anyone in the eyes. This was very odd in a doctor, someone in whose eyes you wanted to search for hope and comfort. He hardly had anything to say unless it was about medicine. When Louise handed him his first cup of tea in our house, she observed that it was a nice day. He said, "Yes," and that was the end of a perfectly good conversation about the weather. Another time she asked him if he liked it here. Another "yes" and his mind drifted off.

I, of course, said next to nothing to the doctor. What was there to say to a man who didn't want to talk back? I respected that about him.

He came to life when anyone asked him a medical question. Then you couldn't stop him. There was the time he went into great detail about the autopsy he did on a body that had been in the water for several weeks. I left the room when he got to the part about the sea lice and the maggots.

Once when he visited our place, soon after the accident, I let my mind wonder if he was a catch. I saw his hand accidentally brush my sister's as she poured his tea. They pulled apart like they'd been scalded and they both turned beet red.

I looked at my dried-up old sister and wondered if she still wanted to marry and have a house full of babies. Time was running out for that dream. And she wasn't getting any help from the old biddies around here, who said marriage for her would be a shame because she was such a good teacher. We had so many teachers who came and went that the parents made a point of trying to tie her down with gifts and kindness. The summers I was four, five and six she had to go back to St. John's to finish some courses so she could be promoted to principal, and all the ladies pitched in and took care of me and Mother. They knew about short-term pain for long-term gain. In my ten years at St. Ann's, I'd seen seventeen teachers come and go. It was a game for us, guessing how long each new teacher would last.

The doctor would have been a poor match for Louise when she was a stunning eighteen-year-old looking forward to a brilliant career. Back then, I imagined, only a handsome, daring man would have won her. But that was past history, a million years ago. Now, though he was at least ten years older than her, they seemed close in age, a bachelor and a spinster, both as dowdy as moths. Two peas in a boring pod.

I started to watch them pretty closely. The last thing I needed before I turned sixteen in June was for Louise to find an escape hatch. I soon noticed that Louise worked extra hard to have our house shining and fresh when Dr. David was expected for a visit. This was the only clue I had that she might be giving his single status—and her own—some thought.

I may not have been smart with the school books, but I was always good at math and I could put one and one together. I would have to do something to put a stop to this nonsense.

IT'S TRUE that I lived in a small place and that I knew absolutely everyone there and everyone knew me. There was no such thing as a stranger in Riverbank. Even a new teacher from the mainland was one of us within a week or two. Yet somehow Wish Sweetapple had come back to the last house tucked around the bend in the lane, the house nearest the clay banks, to live with his grandfather without me noticing. I was still in mourning over Lady at the time and, as I later found out, Wish was helping his sickly grandfather and that kept him close to home. He was no longer the twelve-year-old imp who had been a true friend to me, but an eighteen-year-old, lanky, good-looking boy with dark hair and light-grey eyes that matched his soft sweaters and perfectly pressed flannels.

He jumped back into my life. Literally. He was the brave soul who dived into the icy water and fought with me to save my life. His was the spirit-face I had seen when I surely thought I had died and gone to heaven.

He was the one person who had managed to wiggle his way in between me and my great-aunt when I was a child.

I ONCE HEARD one of my teachers talk about the golden age of the Renaissance. It struck me then that there are times in life when things are good and golden, just right. I had two years like that, from when I was eight to when I was ten. My golden age. Gone before I even realized what happiness was.

It started the first time Wish saved my life. Yes, Wish was an old hand at bringing me back from the brink of death.

It was a June evening. I remember that clearly, because the day was so long that it was almost ten o'clock at night and the sun still hadn't sunk behind the western hills. I was feeling particularly miserable because it was close to my birthday and no one at home seemed to have noticed. Louise usually managed a cake and candles and some kind of gift. I was wearing a white blouse that had just come from the catalogue, but I didn't know if it was meant to be my birthday gift or not. Louise was extremely busy that year because one of the teachers had left early to get married and she was doing two sets of report cards.

I was playing by myself down at the wharf, catching tiny fish on a hook and tossing them to the seagulls, which were starting to get very lazy and saucy. A few of them stopped diving for fish themselves and waited with outstretched wings and squawking beaks for my little catch. It was late before I grew tired of the game of choosing my favourite seagull to feed and imagining he was my very own pet, something my mother and sister would never allow. I especially liked a young chick, still with its brown feathers, that stood back and waited, twisting its neck just a little to catch my eye. Very cute.

No other kids my age would have been allowed to stay out so late. But even at eight I was as free as the very birds I was feeding. Mostly that was because Louise always assumed I was with Lady and Lady assumed I was at home.

To get home from the wharf, I had to pass through a small wood. I had walked through this mangle of dogberry trees a zillion times and it never bothered me. This time, though, I heard something behind me. I turned and listened. I couldn't see anything. The hair stood up on the back of my neck, my body got colder and colder, and I started to shiver. I saw the gleam of something silver edging toward me, but I was rooted to the spot, not a muscle would move, no matter how much I willed it to.

By this time it was pitch-black; the moon had disappeared behind clouds. Another few seconds passed before I found the strength to turn toward the clearing, where I would be safe. That was my undoing. The animal—by now I knew it was probably a dog or a fox—sensed me move and leapt toward me. I felt the paws wrap me in a vise grip, and then a hot, musty breath grazed my cheek. I wanted to scream, but my voice disappeared into my bowels.

The animal pushed me to the ground and its teeth snapped close to my ear. Its jaws opened again, but this time there was another sound—the howl of an animal in horrible pain. It fell back and I scrambled to my feet, moved backward, then stumbled to my knees. I didn't have the strength to save myself. Thank goodness I didn't have to. The boy, Wish, from down the end of the lane was holding a big stick in his hand and the animal was running off into the forest.

"Are you all right? It's Isabelle, isn't it? Isabelle Heffernan?" he said as he helped me up from the ground and brushed me off. "What are you doing out this time of night? Are you okay? Say something, little girl."

It was no surprise that this boy, the boy whom all the children looked to for deciding on summer games and picnics and winter hockey teams and skating parties, would know who I was. Just like I knew he was Wish Sweetapple, though I had never spoken to him.

I still didn't say anything. I was getting over the shock of being attacked and dealing with the double whammy of this second shock, Wish Sweetapple coming to my rescue. He was big and bold and the most popular boy in Riverbank.

"Now I remember," he said. "You're the one who doesn't have a tongue."

I shivered and began to wish the animal had torn me to bits. Pain flickered across my face. I sniffled.

"Look, I'm sorry. I didn't mean to hurt you. I bet you do have a tongue. Here, let me see."

I kept my head down. I could hardly bear the concern and gentleness in his voice.

I felt his hand on my arm. "Come on, I'll make sure you get home okay. That was Moses Butt's dog, the one he usually keeps on a big chain out near his fishing shack. It's no secret around here that when Moses gets drunk, the dog gets a good whipping, and sometimes Moses forgets to feed him or tie him up. People shouldn't be allowed to treat their animals like that. I don't think he'll come back tonight, but you never know how brazen an animal can get when he's half starved," said Wish as he carefully turned my body toward home.

Halfway there, I realized that if I went in and if anyone was up, I'd get a tongue-lashing for tearing another hole in my jeans and having spots of blood on my new white blouse. The last thing I wanted was to make Mother or Louise angry at me yet again. I slowed down, thinking what to do. Then I pointed.

"You want to go to Lady's?"

Wish, a confident boy at eleven, knocked on the door, gentle yet insistent. I remember standing there, knees shaking, the darkness around us, feeling the warmth of his concern.

Lady came to the door and pushed her glasses down her long, thin nose. "Child, my God in heaven, what have you been up to?"

she said as she took in the blood and the tangled hair and the desperation in my eyes.

"Hello, Aloysius, what have you got to say?" said Lady as she pulled me into her tiny hallway. She practically lifted me into her arms and half carried me into her living room and put me down on her old but comfortable couch. Wish trailed in behind us.

"It was Moses Butt's dog, Lady. He jumped her in the dogwood bushes. It was a good thing I was going home. He must have been just behind her. I got him off her and scared him away."

Well, I thought, if I wasn't so shook up, I'd tell Lady a thing or two. Just like a boy to leave out the good parts: about the dog being all black with cold, angry eyes; the dog leaping into the air and landing on me like I was nothing more than a mouse; the big teeth snapping at my ears and burrowing into my hair as the animal looked for something to bite into; the dog's shock when some-thing whacked it across the backside; the yowl when Wish bashed it again and shouted at it to get away.

"My poor, poor darling," said Lady as she went to the window. "I don't see any lights on over at your place. I think you should stay here tonight. Wish, could you slip a note under the door? I'll let them know Issy's here in case someone comes looking."

After Wish left with a crisp white note in my great-aunt's bold black handwriting, she helped me upstairs to the front bedroom, the bedroom that was as familiar to me as the one I shared with Louise across the lane. Even without the note, this would be the first place Louise would look when she didn't find me in my bed in the morning.

"Give me your clothes, sweetheart, and I'll get the blood out of that new blouse and mend your jeans. Get a good night's sleep and you'll be fine in the morning. Your skin hasn't been broken, the blood is from a nosebleed. It's the shock you have to get over. Get all warm and I'll bring you milk and gingersnaps," she said as she helped me into the long, flowery nightdress kept there just for me and examined my head under the lamp. "I don't think we have to bother the doctor, you'll be okay." And with that, Lady picked up my clothes and left me to settle down.

Soon she was back with a tray to set beside my bed. I was already drifting off, curled into the old-fashioned feather mattress, happy in the cozy warmth and wondering why Lady couldn't be my mother—she would be so perfect at it.

"I noticed that you didn't say thank you to that nice boy," Lady said as she sat down on a chair to sew my jeans. "The Heffernans have better manners than that, my dear. Wish was very brave. That dog could have turned on him."

I thought about that and the tears welled up in my eyes.

"Oh, dear, I'm sorry. I didn't mean to upset you. But tomorrow you will have to go to his house and say thank you."

I looked at her, panic in my eyes.

"I have the accounts done for the last church supper. You can bring them to Wish's mother and say what you have to without making a fuss over it. Muriel Sweetapple is about the easiest person to talk to in all of Riverbank," she reminded me.

There was no arguing with Lady. I knew I would have to go for a stroll to Sweetapple Lane, even if it was more frightening than being attacked by a dog.

I WENT OVER to Wish's mom with the pink notebook faintly smelling of Lady's perfume, Tweed, and she hardly noticed that I wasn't one of the kids always bursting in and out of her kitchen. I tried to say thank you to Wish, and as I struggled, turning beet red no doubt, he put his finger to his lips and nodded his head toward his mother. She doesn't know, he was saying. Then he pointed to his watch and cut his hand across his neck. Ah, he wasn't supposed to be out so late himself. He joined his hands as if in prayer, put them back to his lips again and rolled his eyes toward his mom again. Please don't say anything or she'll kill me.

Ah! I had to smile, and while my face glowed with the wonder of playing a little game with Wish Sweetapple, his mother handed me an icing nozzle to decorate a tray of sugar cookies, and that was that. Instantly I was one of his little friends, part of the crowd that followed him around like he was a mother duck with a clutch of waddling chicks. The other children opened up their tight little circle so I could slip through now that Wish had taken me under his wing.

The rest of that year, and the next spring, summer and fall, I went to his house all times of the day and night to sit on the kitchen daybed and watch him doing his homework or helping his mother and father with the chores. Wish and I did all kinds of things together. We fished and went for walks up on the barrens and snared rabbits, and we "borrowed" a boat for trips to the clay banks to get mucky clay for making childish smoking pipes. I trailed after him whenever I saw him alone. He taught me some pretty neat hockey moves, too, once the ice was in for the winter. We would practise together in his little cove where no one could see us. He told me stories about the Beothuk Indians who had disappeared from Newfoundland, and about the Micmac who settled in Riverbank because of the clay banks, the big salmon river that divided us from the rest of the bay and the hunting. He showed me how to find ice-cold spring water, so I only had to carry food on my trips up to the barrens. I think I must have adored him, if that's the right word for an eight-year-old trailing after an eleven-year-old.

Then his parents died and everything changed.

It was December and they were celebrating their fifteenth wedding anniversary. Because it fell on a Saturday, they decided to go to St. Albert's to the Legion for the Christmas dance. Word got back to us later that Wish's mom got up and sang with the band while his dad got everyone out on the dance floor to do the chicken dance. Then they drove their truck to the little landing on the far side of the river. A wind had come up and it began to snow, an early storm that hadn't been in the forecast. They must have decided it was too dangerous to cross the river, so they parked the truck and cuddled up together to keep warm. We know all this because that's how they were found: wrapped in each other's arms in the cabin of the truck, looking very young and like they had gone to sleep for a minute or two. Somehow they had managed to back the exhaust pipe of the truck into a snowbank and they died from carbon monoxide poisoning. I had never heard of such a thing, but it didn't take us too long to learn everything there was to know about that kind of death. We were told it was just like going to sleep, that neither of them felt a thing. And that's what made it almost bearable, knowing they died without pain or torment or violence.

Their leaving us created a big hole in our place. Wish went to stay with his grandfather, his father's father, the two of them the very last of the Sweetapples in our parts, until after Christmas, but then Wish left too. An aunt, his mother's older sister, swooped down and dragged him off to live with her in Toronto. The aunt was quickly labelled a snob when she was heard to say that he could leave all his rags behind, that she would buy him everything new. Somehow she, a girl from our place who finished high school and did training as a secretary, had got herself married to a lawyer in Toronto and apparently that meant they had serious money.

The day before he left, Wish came by my home with a puppy on a thin rope. "He needs a friend," Wish said while he kept his red-rimmed eyes pinned to the ground. It was the little dog his parents had put their dibs in for, from a litter born six weeks earlier in Wabush, Labrador. I named him Bush. Neither Mother nor Louise ever said a word against having the puppy.

Then Wish was gone. He left his entire past behind except for the Sunday-best clothes he was wearing.

Until now. Now Wish was back. Not a little boy anymore, but the same goodness was in his eyes. I saw another look lurking there too, the look that said, "I will help you, little girl." It was a look I'd come to hate. I was past help, but he couldn't know that just then.

A FEW DAYS AFTER the accident, Wish came around to the house to see how Louise and I were doing. I was mortified that a boy close to my own age would see me in my raggedy flannel pyjamas. He thrust his long body into the chair opposite the chesterfield where I was sleeping so my cough would not keep Louise awake at night. By this time my martyr of a sister had gone back to her teaching.

Mother was down the hall. She had not gotten out of bed since the shock of the accident. I don't think it was so much that her only children might have died, but the horror that she might have had to get up out of bed and fend for herself. When she finally spoke to us about the accident, her only words were: "That was a pretty stupid thing to have done, don't you think? I could have been left all alone, and how would I have managed?" And with that, she went back to *Coronation Street.*

Wish glanced down the hallway in the direction of my mother's bedroom. "Is your mother still alive?" he asked, and after a skipped heartbeat I saw the twinkle in his eye. He was joking, but he hit close to the truth too. Mother had barely been outside the house the last ten years. Her kingdom was within our gyproc walls.

Of course, I didn't answer him. I couldn't even look up.

"People told me you were still the shyest creature on earth, but I didn't believe them after the way you swore a rhyme of oaths at me," he said, making a point of looking up under my downcast eyelashes that were hidden by my curtain of hair and my glasses.

I must have turned scarlet. I didn't like it when anyone looked at me close up like that, let alone a boy.

And I was remembering that I did holler at him, using words that would embarrass a sailor. I hadn't wanted to come back up into the cold. I tried to bite his hand, and then I got especially mad when his hand found my ponytail and yanked my hair almost off my scalp.

"You didn't used to be shy with me, remember?" he said as he moved a few inches closer and I moved the blankets further up around my chin. Then his eyebrow went up like a question mark and the memories flooded back to me. Wish was the only person I knew who could raise his left eyebrow like that. He did it all the time when we were kids to make me laugh. Yes, he was right, I had gotten over my shyness with that Wish because he was so sweet and kind and patient.

I also remembered that just when I got to depend on him, he went away. He wrote me a few letters over the years, but I couldn't read them and there was no one I trusted to read them to me. I burned most of the letters in a wicked tantrum because I was so mad at myself for being so dumb.

Now I wanted to ask him all kinds of questions about why he was back, when did he get back, did he know it was me when he risked his life. But I couldn't. The distance was too great, the past too long ago, and he was now a boy. I mean, he was always a boy, but now he was a teenage boy, a good-looking teenage boy dressed like a model in the TV ads for men's suits, a boy all the girls my age would be drooling over and chasing after.

That's when he proved that he was still the kind, gentle boy of long ago.

"It's okay, Isabelle. It'll take a bit of time for you to feel comfortable with me after so many years. But you will, I promise you that. I'll keep coming back until you trust me again. I need a friend, and you were the best friend I ever had," he said as he buttoned up his thick black wool jacket and wrapped a soft blue-grey scarf around his neck.

My chest started feeling better immediately after he left. I couldn't wait to get back to school to listen in on whatever gossip was going around about the new boy in Riverbank.

SERGEANT PAUL FLETCHER decided to investigate the accident himself. Usually a lowly corporal would be assigned to an accident where no one died and no one was at fault. But he had just transferred to the area, was new to his title, and wanted to get out and about and meet the people.

He walked into our living room and clashed with Louise with the first words out of his mouth.

"Would you like a coffee, Officer?" she asked.

"Only if it's fresh and perked, and if you have cream," he answered.

Louise stomped to the fridge for the can of milk, got the jar of instant coffee from the cupboard and quite deliberately put a heaping teaspoonful in the bottom of a mug and splashed in tepid water from the electric kettle while all the time he was watching her.

The book Louise was reading was lying open on the couch and he picked it up. "Who's reading *Gulliver's Travels*?"

Now, that might sound like a reasonable question, but he said it in such a way as to cast doubt on our ability to understand such a thick book with small print. Louise didn't answer him; she abruptly took the book out of his hands and stashed it behind a cushion.

"I imagine you're here about the accident," she said in her school-principal tight voice that was meant to say the meeting would be over when she said so, and sit up straight while we're at it.

He took the mug of coffee from her, sipped it and smacked his lips. "This is the best instant coffee I have ever had," he said as he tried to correct his city ways. Louise sat down stiffly on the narrow wooden arm of the chesterfield and pointed to the chair opposite. The sergeant followed like he was one of her grade three students.

"There's nothing to tell. We got caught by the wind. Everyone is okay. That's the whole story. There's no one to blame and no one to lay charges against," she said with a trace of defiance in her voice.

Sergeant Fletcher took another sip of his coffee and this time had trouble hiding a grimace. He put the cup on the end table and that's where it stayed.

He reached for a notebook and pen and flipped through some pages. "I'm here on another mission, actually. Dr. McKay says you two did a very brave thing coming across the ice with … let me see … Miss Rosalie Peterson … He says you saved her life and that"— he flipped through three pages—"you risked your own lives to save hers. He has put both of your names forward for an award. Each year the RCMP accepts nominations for life-saving awards, and the selections are made in May. You'll probably get your photographs in the papers."

Louise looked at me and I looked at Louise. We were both astonished, and we both knew immediately that I could never stand up in front of a crowd and get an award, never mind having my picture taken.

That's when Louise said she had a spelling test to mark and that she would think about whether we would let our names go forward. She was shooing him out, there was no doubt about it.

"Hmmm … I expected you to be … how do I say it … more interested," he continued. "It's an honour, you know. I'm pretty sure you'll get a certificate of bravery."

I desperately wanted to say something; Louise could see it in my face. As Sergeant Fletcher gathered his stiff Mountie hat and brown leather gloves, she whispered to me, "What is it, Issy? Don't get yourself in a state. Tell me before you have a fit." She would always get a little short-tempered with me when I wouldn't speak up, but she was also the only person who could read my mind. It was so hard to speak with a stranger in the room.

"There's Wish," was all I could manage in her ear. Louise and I had communicated like this for years. I'd say a word or two and she would connect the dots.

"Sergeant Fletcher, if we go forward with the application, you should know there's someone else's name that should be submitted. A young man jumped into the water and saved Issy here. He was the bravest one of all."

"Yes, I have his name down here too." Again he flipped through his notes. "Aloysius Sweetapple of Sweetapple Lane. Odd name that," he said, but then caught the frost in Louise's eyes and cleared his throat to start over. "Yes, I'm on my way to see him too. It would be a separate application, because it was a separate act and he wasn't involved in rescuing young Rosalie," he said, snapping his book shut and almost saluting Louise as he moved toward the door to leave.

"Well, what an arrogant man," Louise said when he was a couple of feet down our garden path. He was well within hearing range, but she didn't seem to care. Louise went to the living room and got the coffee cup and her book. "Imagine not drinking our coffee because it was instant. He's a big-city snob. If he expects to get perked coffee down here, he'd better think again." With that, she threw the coffee down the sink and set her chin in the direction of her room.

I didn't quite know what "arrogant" meant, but I noticed later that he had an air of self-importance whenever he came by in his uniform.

And he seemed to come by a little too often. What was happening? I asked myself. Surely this tall, good-looking RCMP officer wasn't making excuses to see my old prune of a sister? What could he possibly see in her? Sure, she could take down her hair and throw away the glasses for contact lenses and she would look fine, but the sour look on her face would never go away without a kick in the butt.

In my own quiet way, I teased her relentlessly about being an old maid. I'd race home with the news of whatever girl had just announced her engagement, or repeat the rumours about who might be pregnant and who might be getting married real soon. Mostly, her nose would go in the air and she'd leave the room, refusing to join the battle. Never in all my life had I ever heard Louise say she regretted not being married. In fact she seemed to quite enjoy her evenings of knitting and reading once Mother was settled down for the night. The kids from school were not at all encouraged to visit us at home, and once the kitchen was cleaned up, she liked it to stay that way. She talked about leaving us, but she never talked about getting married.

By now Dr. David was seeing Mother every two weeks—the only patient on the whole south coast of Newfoundland that he

made house calls for—and Sergeant Fletcher was busily developing an anti-drug and anti-alcohol program for St. Ann's that
involved meeting with the principal on a regular basis. I kept
telling myself over and over that I was imagining things, that
Louise liked being single, but then I would remind myself that
strange things happen in life. There I was, trying to work up the
courage to tell Mother and Louise that I wasn't going back to
school in September, no matter what, and the ground was shifting
beneath me in subtle ways.

Amid all this heavy thinking I remembered what Sergeant
Fletcher had said about the award for bravery. I couldn't bear to
think about having to stand up in a public place, but then I
thought about Wish. The boy I used to know used to tell me that
everything was possible. Then I reminded myself that "possible"
was a word I couldn't even read.

CHAPTER THREE

Maid: a woman, a young unmarried girl;
frequently used as a term of address

Two days before Christmas, the river was perfectly frozen. It was black and shiny, no chance of it splitting or moving. It didn't always freeze like that, but occasionally the temperature went down at precisely the same time the rain fell, and the winds blew the light snow off the surface. We ended up with the river looking like a ribbon of black, shimmering glass that stretched into the thick ice of the bay. Now that the river ice joined the bay ice, we could skate all the way across the harbour.

My chest was feeling good. Whatever the doctor had given me had worked, and Louise's stitches were mostly healed. She'd taken to wearing her hair more softly to cover the small scar.

The ice from the freezing rain coated our walkway and the laneways too, and I was annoyed that I would likely be trapped in the house all day, the last Saturday before Christmas. I didn't quite feel up to going out and hacking at it. On the other hand, it *was* very pretty. Every tiny branch of the alder bushes was coated in ice that glittered silver in the morning sun. The woods behind our house were a glass forest of white light.

Then the phone rang. I waited for six rings before I approached it. I hated answering the phone. I broke out in a sweat whenever the shrill noise broke our peace. I despised talking into a black plastic thing connected to wires that delivered sound from and into the mists. It so seldom rang in our house, and when it did, it was Louise's job to answer it, especially since I couldn't write down messages. Where was Louise? I could wait all day for Mother to pick it up; the phone wasn't on her "to do" list.

I picked up the receiver and whispered, "Hello."

"That must be Issy," a voice said.

I was puzzled. It wasn't Dad and it wasn't Louise. Who else would know my voice?

"Don't hang up. It's Wish."

I was so surprised, my head jerked up and I cracked my chin on the mouthpiece.

"The river froze solid last night. The horses are out there. They're running up and down in front of my window. I'm getting a crowd together for the Christmas dance over in St. Albert's at the high school tonight. They say if we're bringing a crowd, we need to bring our own chaperone. Could you ask Miss Heffernan if she'll come with us?"

I held the phone in a grip so tight my knuckles hurt.

"She needs to get back on the ice. Tell her I'll be there to help her. You should come too, Isabelle."

My heart was racing and I wasn't sure I could take another breath. Imagine a boy asking me to come to a dance! I said, "I'll tell

Louise," and swiftly hung up. My hands felt like they were burning and I rubbed them until they stopped shaking.

Wish was turning out to be the most sociable person in our place. He and that Beryl Peterson, Rosalie's older sister, who was in my class. I had asked Louise about him after he came by the last time. The story going around was that he'd finished high school early in Toronto and told his aunt he wanted to spend some time in Newfoundland with his grandfather before going to university. The gossip was that his one dream while growing up in Toronto was to come back to Newfoundland. Of course, that was always told with rolling eyes—who would want to come here, when they were up there in Toronto already?

I heard people say when they were remembering Wish's mom that he was like her in every way. She used to be the big organizer in these parts. She would raise money for any charitable cause, from a new altar cloth to shoes for unfortunate children. I remember spending entire evenings making smiley faces on round cookies for some church fundraiser. Wish usually did the yellow icing and I added the black eyes and mouths. The phone never stopping ringing at their place; people called his mother every five minutes to ask her what the Legion would say to sponsoring a bingo, or to get advice on where to borrow money for an air ticket to send a young man to Toronto.

She was also a great country and western singer. People said she could have gone to Nashville. She wrote a beautiful song that she sang hundreds of times the winter she died. It was called "A Beautiful Day," and was about a boy and girl meeting for the first time and then parting and then finding each other again. It was so

pretty, and she made everyone cry when she sang about the darkness of the girl's world all passing away. Wish's home was so different from our silent house. It was as toasty warm as Lady's even
long after the fire in the wood stove went out. I holed up there a
few times to wait out a winter storm.

When Louise came in, I tried to tell her about the phone call,
but she was all upset because of the slippery laneways. She had
been down to the Petersons' general store. "It's miserable outside.
You can't walk a foot without risking your life," she said as she put
a bag of groceries on the kitchen table.

Most people went to St. Albert's for their food or even up to the
big supermarkets in Grand Falls. But not us. We didn't have a car.
Dad was on the boats all the time and Mother had never driven,
even when she was well. Louise got her licence when she was in St.
John's but hardly ever drove. We were probably the Petersons' best
customers. Louise also felt very strongly that we should support
the local businesses.

As I helped put away the groceries, I managed to tell her that
Wish had called about the dance. I didn't tell her the bit about
suggesting I should go too.

"Always in demand, as a chaperone!" she said, slamming the
fridge door shut.

It was true that she was often asked to chaperone dances and
parties. The parents trusted her because she was the principal,
after all, and there were no shenanigans under her watch. She was
also the only teacher at the school who came from Riverbank, and
one of two teachers who wasn't a giddy young woman looking for
a life and using our place as a stepping stone to something better.

Aside from Louise, Miss Simms, my teacher, was the other steady one.

I went to our living room window to see the horses for myself. Their crossing the ice was the signal that the ice was thick and safe. When Louise and I had taken Rosalie across to the ambulance, parts of the river were frozen, but not where the strong current was, close to where the river flowed into the bay.

For the young people of Riverbank, thick ice was the beginning of the dance season across the bay, at the high school. The kids from here were welcome to go to the dances any time, but after crossing the river in a boat it was a twenty-mile trek around the bay, and that meant they had to hitchhike, or else someone had to borrow a car and someone had to stay sober to drive it. Cars were not easy to come by. And even then, no one was sure of getting home because it was very possible that someone else had "borrowed" the boat that had been left tied up and hidden in the bushes for the return river crossing. If the boat was gone, you had to stay on the far shore until someone woke up with a guilty conscience and came for you in the morning. Staying out all night might sound like an adventure, but it was usually a very, very cold one. Twice I'd been out for early morning walks and heard shouts from the far shore. When that happened, I banged on Mr. Jeddore's door and then watched the carousers come back across the water. They were blue with the cold, shivering, teeth chattering.

Once the ice was in, though, you could skate in a straight line down the mouth of our river across the little bay, be in St. Albert's in an hour and not have to depend on anyone.

As we were clearing the table after supper, the phone rang again. This time Louise picked it up.

"Yes, Issy gave me the message … Uh-huh. How many did you say? … Someone will have to come by for me, the lanes are treacherous … I can be ready for eight." She twiddled the curly phone cord and looked at me over her glasses. "Issy doesn't care for crowds. I'll tell her you invited her."

She hung up and smoothed down her apron. "It'll be good to get out of the house for a change. I'll phone Maisy Bennett and tell her to meet me at the Legion after I get the kids settled at the dance. A chaperone is becoming an old-fashioned idea, as I'm sure you know, but the parents here and the nuns at the school won't give up on the notion."

In all honesty, I had no idea of how things were changing and no intention of finding out. Why waste my time and energy on this place, I told myself, when I'd soon be gone?

WISH CAME BY around 7:45 dressed in a dark wool turtleneck sweater and grey flannels under his three-quarter-length black coat. The other boys would be wearing blue jeans and duffle coats; he hadn't been here long enough to know the uniform, or else he didn't care. His long hair curled beautifully onto his shoulders, but a cowlick kept falling into his eyes as he sat at the kitchen table and waited for Louise to finish helping Mother with her nightly bath. I wanted to reach out my hand and press that hank of hair back in place. I was mad at myself when I felt my hand moving on its own across the table, and pulled it back just in time to save myself a great deal of embarrassment. I touched my own hair instead and, as always, it was escaping from its elastic band and wisps of it were everywhere.

"You still have amazing hair, Issy," said Wish, and I immediately shoved my hands in my pockets and hunched down in my chair.

"And you're still as prickly as a porcupine and too shy for your own good," he said so softly I wasn't sure I'd heard him right. "You had better hurry up, just about everyone is down at the shore."

It's hard to come back from a sulk, I'd been in enough of them in my life to know that. But I lifted my head and looked him straight in the eye. I expected to see him laughing at me; instead I saw a gentle young man reaching out to save me from myself. My eyes locked onto his and I knew that "yes" was the only answer he would take. Truth be known, I suddenly wanted to go. I wanted to see what the kids my age did on a Saturday night in our place. I wanted to be with Wish. And, I convinced myself, this would be an opportunity to see how one mixed into a crowd for when I left Riverbank behind forever.

"You won't have to go to the dance, you know, I'll take care of you," he said, and with that I knew I would go. I knew I could never let him down, and based on old times I knew that he wouldn't let me down either. I went to my room to put on warm, sensible clothes.

I'll take care of you. They were the most comforting words I had heard in a long while. And they came from a boy who didn't seem to mind that I wore glasses, had a funny eye and was dead shy. I knew my dad *meant* to take care of me, but he was always gone. Yes, he sent most of his paycheque home every month to Louise, but it would have been much better if he could have found a job here. Even if jobs were scarce, he was clever enough to find a way to keep us clothed and fed.

As soon as we were outside, Louise clung to Wish so she wouldn't fall. At the shore, we met up with ten others, put on our skates and set off. No one seemed to notice me in the pack. Except Wish. He was true to his word. No matter how many of the other boisterous girls grabbed his arm, no matter how many times Beryl Peterson and Diane Smith called out to him, I could feel he was watching me as I stayed in the background, never calling attention to myself.

Everything was a barrel of laughs until someone up front shouted, "Open water, maids, the coastal steamer's cut a path." We stopped in a huddle, and in the wink of an eye a couple of boys skated to a tiny, hidden beach and came back dragging an aluminum rowboat. I caught on right away. The trick was to jump the ice pans like I did as a kid until we could launch the boat, and then to jump into the boat, row across the thirty yards or so of open water where the steamer had cut a path, jump ice pans on the other side until we gained solid ice again, and then tuck the boat away when everyone was across.

I was a little scared at first, and so was Louise. We both knew how unforgiving the cold water could be. But Wish helped Louise into the boat and then came back for me. No one else noticed or sensed any possible danger. Most of the girls fell into the boat in a giggling fit, bottoms first and skates over the side so they'd be ready to jump out again. Everyone was laughing, as if they'd done this complicated manoeuvre a hundred times. I couldn't help but laugh along with them once I felt safe. Louise somehow managed

to sit up in the boat and keep her back straight, like a school principal should.

When we got across the bay, we exchanged our skates for the
boots we'd carried with us, and the first stop for the girls was the
bathroom to repair makeup and take off snow pants and woollen
sweaters. So far it had all been fun, but suddenly I didn't know
what to do with myself.

"Maid, your sister and Wish are waiting outside for you," said
one of the girls, and I left the bathroom quicker than a bolting
moose.

Wish was lounging against the wall, smoking a cigarette, looking
like a cross between the clean-cut Frankie Avalon and the rock star
Mick Jagger. Louise was speaking to several spinster-type women,
the kind who still had Toni perms every month to make their hair
crinkly. She turned to me when I came out of the ladies' room.

"Look, Issy, I can't see why you came. I told you that you could-
n't cling to me. As soon as all the kids are in the gym, I'm going to
the Legion for an hour. I told you I had that all set up."

I wanted to cry, even though I knew I was too big to cry and I
would never be able to show my face in public again if I cried at
my first dance. I knew already that I couldn't cling to Louise, but
the least she could have done was to tell me gently and kindly, not
in that cold, hard voice in front of her friends and, well, Wish too.

I put up a fist to hide the tears that were lacing my eyelashes.

"What say you and I meet up with everyone after the dance, my
dear," said Wish as he eased into my line of vision and steered me
away from Louise. "I have an old great-aunt here who makes a
wonderful cup of tea. She would love to meet you."

I hated meeting anyone, but this was far better than having to hide out at the dance. My eyes shifted to Louise.

"She won't even notice we've left," Wish said as he crushed out his smoke and guided me toward the stairs and out the front door of the high school.

"COME IN, COME IN, my boy. My dear Aloysius, you never come often enough. Let me take a look at you. Who have you got there? You've never brought a friend these past weeks," said an elderly woman with a rosy complexion, though her skin was paper-thin. Her white hair was piled on her head in an old-fashioned bun and she had a very straight back.

"This is Isabelle Heffernan. She's from over our way. She's in grade nine and will be coming over to St. Albert's to school next September. Isabelle, this is my great-aunt Euphemia."

"You're the only one who calls me that, my boy. You're Lady's kin, aren't you, maid? Call me Effie. She and I were friends back a long time ago. I didn't think my brother would let you go around with the Heffernans," she said as she caught Wish's eye.

Wish opened his eyes wide in puzzlement and his left eyebrow shot up. I too was surprised.

"Grandfather has never said anything about the Heffernans. He has never said anything about any of my friends," said Wish as he eased me toward the cozy little living room.

Even though Wish's grandfather was an angry old man, I couldn't think of any time that he had bothered me. Certainly Lady had not mentioned any family feud when she sent me off to say thank you that time after the dog attacked me.

Great-aunt Effie's face brightened. "In that case, come in, child, and sit down. Come in, come in, for sure," she said as she plumped the flowered cushions on her living room couch. "I can see the Heffernan turned-up nose and rosebud mouth. You missed out on the red hair of your lot, but black against your pale colouring looks lovely—not as pretty as your great-aunt was, but maybe a bit more interesting," she said, and then changed course before I could take in her backhanded compliment. "You look too big for the grade nine."

I took a deep breath, but Wish must have been saying something with his eyes or hands behind my back for she quickly changed her tone.

"Oh yes, I remember now. Your mother is ill. I hear you and your sister are tied to her bedpost. I imagine that's what's keeping you at home," said Great-aunt Effie with a frankness that told me she certainly was not shy.

Ah, I thought, that's one of the stories that's going around about me and Louise. Either Great-aunt Effie hadn't heard the one about how I was too dumb to graduate from the elementary school or she was too nice to bring it up at our first meeting. I was given a cup of tea and asked to do nothing more than what I liked doing most—listening—while Great-aunt Effie talked about the old days. It turned out she was Wish's grandfather's only sister and that she and Lady had been friends from their first day at school.

"We didn't see each other much after the war. I mean the *First* World War. It was so hard to get across the bay. We didn't have cars back then, or even telephones. And it wasn't proper for a school-teacher like me to keep a boat.

"We were all so surprised when Lady went overseas, and then even more surprised that she'd come back after practically being secretary to the prime minister of England."

I loved hearing about Lady, and Great-aunt Effie could talk the ear off a sow. All you had to do was wind her up.

"I have a wonderful photo here somewhere of her. Let me see if I can put my hand on it," said Great-aunt Effie as she reached for a photo album that was beautifully organized. "Yes, here it is. It was done by a photographer in England when she went to a big country house party."

I reached for the album and pushed my glasses to the angle I knew I'd need to see the photo. Lady was all in white, possibly white lace, with a white lace headband cutting across the straight hair on her forehead. She looked like a china doll and was standing at the base of a big circular staircase.

"Lady and I had lots of good times, then the Great War happened and I got a job teaching here, and my brother—well, that's another story for another time. She sent me this photo to show me the latest styles in London so I could copy the dress. I still miss having her as my best friend. It all seems like only yesterday. She was the smartest person I ever knew and so generous," she said as she stirred her tea, stared off into the distance and for a moment forgot we were in the room as she rummaged through her past.

At eleven-thirty, after four cups of strong India tea and a plate of melt-in-your-mouth shortbread cookies, Wish said we had to go. At the door, Great-aunt Effie waved us off and told Wish to bring his girl any time. I didn't know where to turn, so I shoved my hands in my pockets, put my head into my chest and walked at a fast trot back to the school, totally ignoring Wish. We gathered in the school porch and did a head count; this would not be a good time to leave anyone behind. Louise came out of the Legion across the road with her friend Maisy, and behind them was that Mountie, Sergeant Fletcher—not in his uniform, of course, but even in the darkness I could pick out his height and the way he walked, like he was wearing a Stetson even when he wasn't. I caught a bit of their good nights on the crisp night breeze.

"Thank you, Sergeant, but I know my way home. It's kind of you to offer to drive a few of us, but really, we enjoy the skating."

Even I knew that was a brush-off, though I'd never heard a brush-off before in my life.

We were a quiet group as we headed down to the beach to put on our skates. More than a couple of the girls and guys had sneaked some liquor at the dance, and Wish took charge of getting them to join in a singalong so we would stay together as we crossed the ice. Getting us all in a rowboat on skates was scarier than when we came over, but all hands were accounted for by the time we hid the boat again. Some of the girls were starting to sober up, and three or four of them hitched a ride in train fashion with Wish.

It was a night with a purple-black sky and a big, pale moon. The stars were pinpoints of white light twinkling in the blackness. I was happy skating after midnight with Wish keeping an eye on me. I wasn't the least bit tired.

Then it all crashed down around me. I had just helped pretty, kind Beryl Peterson untie her laces when Diane Smith came over to me and whispered drunkenly in my ear, "Don't get any ideas about Wish, Dizzy-Issy. Beryl's got her eye on him, you know. He's only being nice to you because he knows you're a sad case. Guys don't make passes at girls who wear glasses."

Wish came up to me as Diane finished talking. He had a wide grin on his face that told me he hadn't heard. He had been helping one of the young guys throw up his potato moonshine a good piece away. Louise had gone ahead and was waiting for me near the government wharf. I turned on my heel and walked quickly toward her. At least I had been saved the mortification of Wish and Louise hearing what everyone was thinking.

CHAPTER FOUR

Mug-up: a cup or mug of tea and a snack taken
between any of the main meals

Christmas was a truly awful time in our home. It had been like that all my life. There was overtime work to be had on the boats over the holidays and Dad took as much of it as he could get. We always seemed to have enough money for the things we needed, so it was never clear to me why he worked more than he had to. Dad showed up for a day or two during the festive season, but those days could fall any time between December 24 and old Christmas day, January 6. He seemed to be more connected to his crew than to his family, and he shipped out just as soon as it was decent to go.

Then again, Christmas was when Mother was at her worst.

Some of my earliest memories are of Mother going in and out of the hospital. When I was very young, she'd had at least half a dozen episodes, or "attacks," as she liked to call them. I'd hear bits of conversation about whether or not Mother was going to pull through. I got this image in my head of my mother shrinking up like a bit of silk handkerchief and being pulled through the eye of a needle. If the doctors could pull her through, she would live. I had nightmares over and over of bits of coloured ribbon and silk floating from the sky and smothering me in my bed.

Now my nightmares were about being clumsy and dropping trays and breaking tea sets. All my life Mother had been a tyrant about what chores had to be done and by what time. She gave the orders from her bed or, on a good day, from a corner of the living room couch in front of the TV.

First it was breakfast in bed, served to her on a big tray with fold-down legs that she'd bought in Halifax, where my family lived when Louise was a child. The tray had to be covered in white Irish linen, perfectly starched and ironed, a clean cloth every day. We had a special oversized drawer that Dad built in the kitchen for this linen and for the matching napkins, which were folded just so in perfect rectangles, pressed but with no creases showing.

The teacup had to be part of the china set that matched the white-and-green teapot, sugar bowl and milk jug. Louise said the set was very special because it was made in Ireland, was very expensive and was the first thing Mother bought as a married woman. Both Louise and Mother thought it the finest china on earth and called it Belleek. Mother said her parents liked to collect antiques, but she had wanted something new and pretty. Thank goodness the set had made it through more than thirty years of hand washing and drying without a chip or a crack. Louise and I knew that life would be a constant whine if any piece ever broke, and we were very careful handling each teacup and plate. Along with the strong tea, Mother had to have two slices of evenly toasted bread set in a silver toast rack that gleamed with constant polishing.

It wasn't the tea and the toast that was the bother. No one would begrudge her mother a rest in bed and a cup of tea, even if this went on for fifteen years. It was the fact that she never appreciated an ounce of the work that had to be done to get the tray to her bedroom. If Louise was a minute late, or the tea wasn't hot enough, or the toast was too light or too brown, or the tea had sloshed on the way to her room, she'd notice right away and have a charming word ready, like, "Why can't you get this right? It's one small thing that I ask and here it is, another disaster."

She was especially hard on me because I couldn't ever get it right. Mostly, I was banned from her bedroom unless there was no one else to do her bidding. To make myself useful—and we all had to be useful to her—I did the heavy outside chores: shovelling a path to the gate in the winter, banging the icicles off the eaves, clearing the snow off the roof, carrying the heaviest bags up from the shop, catching and gutting fresh fish, dumping the garbage, planting and weeding the flower garden and the potato patch— anything where a little muscle was needed. I was just as keen to do the outside work as Mother was to get me out of the house, so it did in fact work out in some harmony.

She was also a master at keeping emotions on edge. I remember well a time when Dad didn't get her the gift she wanted for Christmas. As a treat he took me to Grand Falls with him to do some business and to help him buy a special present for Mother. I was very patient while Dad took ages to look at every nail and screw in the hardware store. And I didn't complain as he demonstrated power drills for me or took a full hour to go over outboard motors for a boat we didn't own. After that, he bought me french fries and steered me toward the one jewellery store in town. The problem, I noticed when Dad bought me the fries, was that he was out of money. He'd used his cash to buy a fancy new hand drill and was down to a twenty-dollar bill. And, he explained, we still needed to buy gas at the Irving station for the trip back.

I knew for certain that my mother expected a particular gold charm. She was very fond of her charm bracelet. She wore it all the time, even when she didn't get out of bed. Most of the mothers in our place wore silver bracelets with little squares or circles engraved with their children's birthdates or marking a child's special accomplishment. A scroll or a graduation hat meant someone in the family had made it through high school, and the mother broadcast this fact proudly on her bracelet. Not my mother. Her charm bracelet was all about her. Her charms were ordered from catalogues she spent hours poring over. She talked on and on about her map of England, a miniature Tower of London, an X for her school, St. Francis Xavier for Girls, a sewing machine for when she used to sew all her own clothes, a square with her birthdate on it, November 20, 1918, and her horoscope sign, Scorpio. Mother was fond of pointing out that her charms were a mix of 22-karat and 14-karat gold, depending on whether she ordered them from Europe or from Birks in St. John's. The shiniest of all, the one she was most fond of, was a gold airplane with a speck of a diamond on each wing. I often wondered if it reminded her of how much easier it was to cross the Atlantic now than when she came over on the *Queen Mary*. Louise would often say that the airplane was her favourite too.

We usually had to guess what Mother wanted as a surprise gift, and if we got it wrong, she'd have an excuse to pout for a week. For her birthday that November she had wanted a matching bed set, a nightdress and a bed jacket. The catalogue was left open—accidentally, of course—at a certain page one evening. Dad didn't pick up the hint and got her a pair of sealskin slippers. She was upset for the rest of his visit and wouldn't tell him why. Once the penny dropped, Dad, who hated to upset Mother, came up with the plan to make it up to her at Christmas with the charm Louise and I thought she wanted.

The trick always was to figure out what was on her mind, and it was a treacherous game that she won most of the time. The rules were unclear. The first one seemed to be that the less Mother said about something, the more she wanted it. Louise was the one who noticed how Mother had jangled her bracelet when the Queen was on the news with her dogs. We knew all about Mother's dainty little childhood Precious, a Welsh corgi just like the Queen's, because she was forever comparing him to my gawky, overweight Bush.

The nice man in the jewellery store was grand at first about taking out a tray of charms and pointing out two Welsh corgis. He took out the expensive charms first, the ones my mother liked. I stood a little separate from Dad as he rested his elbows on the glass and kept his eyes focused on the velvet tray. Even though I was just a kid, I knew this was not going to end well. My dad was never one for saying much, but some silent communication passed between the salesman and Dad, and the charms got thinner and smaller as we moved away from the 14-karat gold to the 10-karat gold and all the way to silver plate. Then their voices got all stiff, the words were almost non-existent, and the salesman pinched his lips and looked around for an excuse to shoo us out.

We left the jewellery store empty-handed. Dad didn't seem to care and was whistling "Henry the Eighth I am, I am."

The next stop was the Woolworth store, where Dad had me pick out a small tea tray. I chose the one with flowers growing up around the banks of a small bubbling brook. It looked like the English countryside I saw on TV and very different from the bombed-out cities Mother talked about. The tray was too small for the kind of tea we served our mother, but at $5.98 it was well within Dad's budget.

Mother hated the tray. "Where did you get something this awful?" were the first words out of her mouth when she opened the package I'd carefully decorated.

I couldn't tell if Dad heard her. He'd lost a good bit of his hearing when he was a gunner in the war, and he missed a lot of things. Or only half heard them. Or didn't hear when it was convenient not to hear. Whatever he felt about Mother, he didn't tell us. We knew to expect that when things got rough, he'd be going back to work a bit early. There was always someone off sick, you see, or someone who needed to be home with the family more than he did. Our lot was no different from that of many families here, where the men went off logging for months on end, or on the trawlers for six months at a time, or to Ontario to work long enough to collect unemployment insurance.

The second rule in handling Mother was not to let her see how it hurt. I would save and save and hope I got it right this time. But

I never did. Every special occasion was the same. Louise or I would give her a gift and an anxious smile and she would open it and say, "Oh dear, girls, I know I said I wanted a nylon head scarf, but you must know that pink is my absolute worst colour." Or, "These earrings would be perfect if they weren't so small." Or so big or so whatever.

We got to dread opening gifts in our house.

This Christmas proved to be no different. Because of the accident and because it felt good to be alive, I tramped a good two miles into the woods on Christmas Eve to find a lovely tree. I got the tree every year, but, knowing no one cared what it looked like, I usually didn't put much effort into it. This time I got us a perfect fir, even branches all around, six feet high. I brought it out over the snow on a sleigh and decorated it myself with the glass and silvery ornaments we kept in the shed.

Mother puffed her way out to the living room on Christmas morning, took one look at the tree and said, "Last year's was so much better, don't you think?" She did have a charming way with words.

A couple of days later Dr. David mumbled that it was the prettiest Christmas tree he had ever seen, and Wish came by with a gift of a stack of kindling for our backup wood stove and said it was the best tree in Riverbank. Their kind words took the bite out of Mother's sting.

MOST ALL OF the other families visited back and forth throughout the year. The women often had tea and coffee together in the afternoons once the chores were done, where they sewed or knitted and gossiped. The talk was mostly about when the men were coming home and what the women planned to buy with the next cheque: new shoes, a furnace, a stove, coats for the winter. Children in our place were in and out of everyone's back door, and any of the mothers would make up a sandwich or put out a couple of cookies for a hungry child. Everyone, that is, except us. There were no shared secrets in our bedrooms, no giggling girls. Dad had his boyhood friends who visited with him down at the Petersons' shop when he was home, but none of them ever came to our kitchen for a mug of tea. It was known in our place that Mother needed quiet, and quiet she got.

After the accident, however, things changed. The doctor decided that Mother could get better (little did he know that she didn't want to get better), and he came through our door with a white light of hope flickering just over his shoulders, where I always imagined an angel would be. He was in our kitchen after every visit, nibbling on the tips of the wedge-shaped scones fresh out of the oven or doing up his paperwork as he waited for someone to take him back across the river. Sometimes Louise would fuss and ask him if he wanted some supper, and sometimes she would sit across from him at the kitchen table as she did her school reports.

That Mountie, Sergeant Fletcher, found more papers to write up about the accident and came by quite regularly to ask for more details and to get signatures on papers.

And Wish. We couldn't keep him away. I tried for a while, but without any luck. I went to my bedroom whenever he came in the kitchen door. Or I would accidentally rattle Bush's leash and he would go nuts, like I knew he would, and wouldn't let off until I put on my coat and left with him. Once Wish said he would come with me, but Bush, ever a loving and faithful dog, snarled at him with bared teeth, and Wish knew it was best if he stayed put. Another time I pointed toward my mother's bedroom and rushed down the hall. As much as I liked Wish, I figured he was just feeling sorry for me. He thought he could save me like he did when I was eight years old, but I knew I was beyond redemption. I was the stupidest girl in Riverbank and there was no way on earth he could smarten me up. Besides, I had a plan, and part of that plan was to stick to my plan.

It was around this time that Beryl Peterson, a girl who used to be a grade behind me and whom I ignored like I did everyone else at school, floated by my desk one day when there was no one else around and whispered, "Issy, you need to get to work. You're never going to pass grade nine without help. You are in serious trouble. I don't mind giving you a hand."

She wasn't the only one who noticed. My teacher, Miss Simms, who was in her fourth year at the school, tried to help too, but I hunkered down behind my hair if she so much as made a step in my direction.

Louise hadn't said another word about trying to teach me to read after the flash cards. That session ended like all the others, in a big fight, with her telling me I was not trying and me chalking up another failure. In the past I'd run to Lady, but this winter I had no one to listen to me about my family troubles. I certainly couldn't burden Wish; he had enough on his plate taking care of his elderly and ill granddad.

At first I figured Beryl, by far the sweetest girl in our school, was being kind to me only because I had helped save her little sister's life. Perhaps that's when she first noticed me. I sat at the back of the class when I went to school, and I didn't bother to go to school at all whenever the weather was nice or I didn't feel like it. But it didn't take a genius to figure out she had a crush on Wish; and since Wish seemed intent on gluing himself to me, she needed to be on my good side. It was crystal clear that she was making a play for him by using me. I was willing to go along with this because I knew Wish was delusional if he thought he and I would ever be a couple. He needed a smart, pretty girl like Beryl. And sometimes a tiny voice reminded me that no matter what I did, knowing how to read would make life a lot easier. If I went up to Toronto, how would I manage? Sometimes I half frightened myself to death with my plans.

As hard as it was going to be, though, my mind was made up. I was easing off on helping the shy kids in the playground, and was going to see Mrs. John and Mildred less and less, so they wouldn't miss me all at once.

Wish, meanwhile, was getting more attached to Riverbank as each week went by. He was coaching some of the little boys in hockey, and he was walking door to door with a petition to the government in Ottawa to help the people who were descended from the Micmac Indians, who had settled here lifetimes ago. They were asking for special status so they could get the same government money as other Native people in the rest of Canada. He was wedging himself right in.

But there was no way he was going to hold me back.

One cold morning while I was visiting with Lady up in the cemetery, I decided that if Beryl could help me to learn to read, then the both of us would get closer to what we wanted.

THE PETERSONS were the family that gave our place some class. Along with the shop and the hunting and fishing lodge, they had the first black-and-white TV in Riverbank and then the first colour set; they had the fastest boat on the river and the biggest house, with dormer windows upstairs and two bay windows downstairs bookending a wide front porch.

They also had a "girl." Mrs. Peterson took a great deal of time to train each girl and was always upset when, within a year, the girl went off to be married. Mrs. Peterson hadn't cottoned on to the fact that her girls were in big demand with the male set. It was well known that after Mrs. Peterson trained them, the girls could cook interesting and strange foods and make a comfortable and pretty home. The women who kept flowers in window boxes and white lace curtains on their living room windows were usually former "girls."

My mother had never liked Mrs. Peterson. She was too uppity, my mother would say. Well, I guess she knew what that was all about. Mrs. Peterson worked tirelessly and cheerfully from dawn to midnight. It took more than one "girl" to keep a house sparkling, hot meals on the table and a family of five children neat and tidy. Even the two boys wore pressed shirts and creased grey flannels to school every day. My mother, on the other hand, had not wasted one second of her life worrying about whether I had eaten my breakfast or if I combed my hair for school.

Beryl was the eldest, and there were two younger brothers and two sisters, one of them Rosalie. The younger sisters and brothers were sent home to bed the moment they had a slight sniffle. Dr. David got into the habit of going to their place when he came over to see my mother, because he knew that at least one Peterson child was sure to be sick.

Beryl was different. She was wholesome. If she got sick, you knew she was *really* sick. She hated to be fussed over. Once I got to know her a little, I could tell she was annoyed about how coddled her sisters and brothers were.

At first I pushed Beryl away. Sure, I wanted a friend my own age, but I was also afraid of having ties that bound me to Riverbank. The easiest thing to do was to act like I wasn't interested. I refused the molasses raisin cookies she baked and brought to school for our class. I turned away from her when she sat beside me in the playground at recess. She fed Bush treats, and the idiot ate them up and pressed for more with his big, sad eyes.

But she was relentless, thank goodness. We had next to nothing in common. She was the most popular and the youngest girl in our class; I was older than everyone else in grade nine and felt alone. She was smart; I was dumb. She dressed in the clothes her mom bought her in the big malls in St. John's—little minidresses that barely covered her behind, bell-bottomed trousers and lacy see-through blouses, a lot of black like the beatniks, and occasionally a splashy rainbow-coloured tent dress or tight skirt showing her long, muscled legs and curves. I wore the same faded, ragged jeans and sweaters made by Lady from long-ago patterns for weeks and weeks. The only way I knew anything was in fashion was when

Beryl showed up wearing it. I also knew I would look like a cow if I tried to dress like her.

I was secretly fascinated by Beryl. She was a big-boned girl like me, but she carried her height and wide shoulders with confidence. There was no slouching or embarrassment because she was bigger than all the boys in our grade, just a childish joy that she could beat them at almost any sport, even ice hockey. She stood out in any crowd because, while she had golden hair like all the Petersons, hers had a white curly streak, the thickness of a finger, that sprang from the middle of her hair part and swept down the side of her face. If she had been a movie star, you would have assumed it was fake because it was so unusual. But those who knew her from when she was a baby swore that the stark white curl had been the first to grow.

Beryl was the one who spoke up first in our class. If Miss Simms asked a question, even something as simple as, "Would anyone like to help decorate for St. Patrick's Day?" I would bury myself deeper in my desk and use my hair and books as camouflage. Not Beryl. She'd slowly raise her hand and look around to see who else was responding. If anyone else's hand was up, she'd lower hers with a warm smile, kind of saying, "Hey, you take this one." If hers was the only hand, as it often was, she'd look around and with her eyes include the whole class, and then she'd answer for all of us. "Yes, Miss, we'll form a group to help with the decorations. We can start tomorrow." And so it was done. A cluster would gather, names would go on a piece of paper, and the decorating, or the bake sale to buy candles for the church or food for the orphans in Africa or to raise money for the March of Dimes, would be organized.

I had never been on her team. She had never asked me to help
with anything. And now that I was watching her for clues, I saw for
the first time that she was so kind and giving that anyone could be
on her team; all you had to do was get close to her and you were
included. She didn't single people out—they shoved each other
aside to get close to her.

One dreary day in January, while we were putting on our coats
in the cloakroom, Beryl grabbed me by the sleeve and wouldn't let
go. "I want so much to help you, Issy," she said. "You saved our
Rosalie's life and my whole family wants to do something for you,
but you won't let anyone get close. Please let me help you with
your homework. My mom would be so happy."

Ah, I thought, that's what she wants me to believe. I nodded.
Somehow Beryl had already worn me down, and there was no way
I was going to escape her good intentions. If she wanted Wish in
exchange for the help, so be it. It was more than a fair bargain, I
thought, because I would be giving something I didn't even
want—someone I would be leaving behind soon enough.

I'D ALWAYS HAD TROUBLE with books. I wore these ugly glasses
that constantly slipped down my nose and were almost as big as
my face. They certainly helped me to see far into the distance, but
they didn't make much difference when I opened a book.
Whatever the other kids saw when they looked at a page was a total
mystery to me.

The teachers didn't pick me out as being different the first few
years in school. I was a good listener and could answer all the
questions if the teacher read out loud. But the teachers stopped

reading the stories and textbooks aloud when I got to the higher grades. Then they called me a slow learner and I was left alone to daydream. By the time I was seven or eight, I would get up a good howl when I couldn't do some little thing that all the other children learned in seconds. The teachers didn't know what to do with me, and turned a blind eye when I ran away to the barrens to spend a happy day walking, fishing or berry picking. I didn't go far at first, but I went farther and farther as I got older. No one noticed or cared when I skipped school to go wandering. Except Wish. Before he went away, he was always after me to try harder, to not run away from school. In a nice way. Not preachy, like a certain sister. But then he left and I sank back into my bad habits.

Louise tried to teach me when I was a youngster, I'll give her that, but as I got older she would often say to me, "No one can help someone as stubborn and slow as you are, my dear." The "my dear" softened it a little, but there was no doubt what she really meant. She constantly accused me of refusing to learn my books. I was the sister who drove her beyond crazy because I did not meet her expectations.

None of the kids my age ever let me play with them when I was in the lower grades. Somehow I never understood the invisible rules. We'd all join a circle to start some game and more often than not I went in the wrong direction. Or they'd pass notes back and forth under the desks; I was left out of that game entirely. Some of the kids at school called me Dizzy-Issy, though not often to my face.

School was a real nuisance. I got antsy as soon as I smelt the chalk. I stared out the window and never heard a thing unless it was the bell for the end of class. The teachers, one after another, all thought they could save me from my failures. They tried to get me to hold my head up, to stand tall, to look at them, to take the hair out of my eyes, to speak up, to read. But not one of them made any difference. They were all from away, passing through our place in search of a paycheque, teaching experience, a husband and a good time. They seldom touched our hearts. I didn't give them the time of day. I liked Miss Simms, but she came along far too late for me.

I wasn't so dumb that I didn't know I had to try one more time to learn to read. I was listening real hard to people saying how they took the bus in Grand Falls to Port aux Basques, and after the ferry they got on a train, then changed in Moncton and changed again in Montreal, and you got off at Union Station and there was an underground subway system that took you anywhere you wanted to go in Toronto. I had patched all of this together and worried my way through it as I stared out the window at school. The problem was, how would I know what train to get on, what subway to take, where to get off if I couldn't read any of the signs? Dad had mentioned once that dogs were allowed on the ferries, but I didn't know if dogs were allowed on the buses and trains.

I needed Beryl's help far more than she knew.

I SOMETIMES FELT SORRY for my old maid of a sister, but not sorry enough to end up like her—a prisoner of her own inertia in a dreary house in a nothing town miles from everywhere.

While my sister and I had our problems, we also had a history together. She was the one who walked the floor with me through my bouts of earache and measles and mumps. I'm told that babies don't remember that far back, but I can verify they do when it's all about pain and dread. She once told me how she was the first one to take me for walks up on the coastal barrens, to get away from the children who teased ruthlessly.

I would be lulled by these stories from my past, but then she would throw her punch. "I know those days were hard, but you know, we all have to get on with life and we have to take what life gives us and make the best of it."

That's when the conversation was over. Ten-four, over-and-out. The last thing I needed was a sister as sour as lemons telling me to buck up and get on with things.

After the accident I often went to sleep remembering Louise telling me to save myself. That must have taken some guts and some selflessness. But I also took it to heart: maybe it *was* time to save myself. And maybe the way to save myself was to climb on the back of the reading monster and conquer it once and for all.

CHAPTER FIVE

Cruise: to go around on foot; to look for game
or some object; a visit with relatives or friends

Mother squeezed her eyes closed when she saw my Christmas report card, and her eyebrows shot up to her hairline. I think if she could have jumped out of bed she would have whacked me. Not a whack to knock me senseless, but one to knock some sense into me. I had got my marks the last day before the holidays, but I "lost" the report card until late January, when Louise stuck her nose into my affairs.

"Mother, did you see Issy's report card? It's shocking. Something really has to be done with that girl," Louise said while getting Mother her bedtime tea on Saturday.

I was sent to find it and after a few minutes of looking, lo and behold, there it was under the breadbox in the kitchen.

Usually Mother didn't care what I did or where I went as long as all the heavy work was done and she could read one of her Harlequin romances in peace. But she took an unusual interest in end-of-term marks, and my report card was a lightning rod for her anger every time.

When Louise was going through school, her exam results must have been a bond between them. Mother had often found ways to tell us that while she was at school in England she was at the top of her class. She expected the same of Louise, and Louise had come through for her.

Now, my report card had never been a thing of beauty. I got A's in everything in kindergarten, but by the time I was in grade two, Mother would "tut, tut," over the marks. Back then she really was too sick to help me or to care very much. And Louise was busy taking care of Mother and me and the house, doing a full-time job and studying by correspondence to finish university.

Mother scanned the Christmas report card and puckered her lips. Louise stood by her side with her arms hugging her chest.

"Why don't you just quit school now? It seems to be a waste of time. There's a lot of work you could be doing here," said Mother.

"She's not sixteen, Mother, and won't be until June. You know the government rules, and I am the principal," said Louise, all in a huff.

I kept my head down with the hair over my face so they couldn't see my half smile.

"Go to your room, Isabelle," said Mother. "Louise and I will talk about what to do with you. You're a disgrace to the Heffernan name. I'll never get well or leave this house if I have no reason to hold up my head."

I waited in the darkness for what seemed like hours. I could hear Louise and Mother talking in Mother's room, but I couldn't make out the words. Bush could tell I was restless and he kept his ears cocked toward the door the whole time.

Finally Louise came in, got undressed in the dark and slipped between her cold sheets.

"I know you're awake, Issy, but there's nothing to tell you. Mother is very upset. You are not trying. I am upset too. How do you think I feel as a teacher when I'm not able to teach my own sister? I've been trying to figure out how to help you for years, and the more I think about it the more I think you need some professional help. They have special programs in bigger places for people like you. I know I've called you stupid many times, but you're not—not at all. I've been watching you over the years. You can learn whatever you want, so long as it's not in a book."

Well, this was news to me. Not stupid? How dare she say that! It was the one thing about me that I knew to be true, that I could hang on to, that kept me from utter despair. If I wasn't stupid, why couldn't I learn?

"There's something not connecting in your head," said Louise in the darkness.

"Don't go making things up, Louise," I whispered back. "I know I'm stupid and dumb and hopeless. I know my limitations. Don't go telling me I can do something that's impossible."

That's when she got out of bed and came over and shook me. Bush jumped on the bed beside me and bared his teeth at her. She snarled back at him and he settled down.

"Maybe you're dumber than I think. What I see is a girl who can do whatever she wants to do. You've proven this over and over. You learned your math with Lady, didn't you? You know how to do hundreds of things around this house that I could never do.

"Remember the time you fixed the gas generator? What about the time you figured out how many tiles we'd need after that storm blew off half the roof shingles? And the time when you were six and you found Dad's wallet when he left it up at the church. You told us you thought about where he'd been and then walked right to it. Then you found the hidden beach out at the coast and marked out a path to it so we could all go. When you were ten, your teacher told me that you could rhyme off the prime ministers of Canada better than anyone in the class.

"Perhaps you choose not to learn. That's what I think. I think you're refusing to learn to read because something else is going on. Maybe you don't want to leave Riverbank and go to the high school across the bay. Maybe you don't want to leave Mother ..."

That's when a long, low, nervous giggle escaped from the back of my throat.

"I didn't think that was the reason, but one never knows. Here's something you should know: I am going to leave. I can't take it anymore. I'm almost thirty-five years old and I've got to get on with my plans. I want to teach at the university level, not a bunch of crybaby kids. I want to see the world. I'm nothing but a maid to Mother, a convenience to Dad and of no help to you whatsoever. I'm the eldest and I get no respect and no thanks for giving up all the things I've had to give up for this family. I was not much older than you are now when you were born. I had to grow up fast, and you need to too.

"Dad didn't even think to give me Lady's cross. She promised it to me and it should have been mine. I'm just a pair of hands and another paycheque," said Louise as she held my shoulders tight and kept my eyes even with hers, our faces much too close.

I couldn't figure out when the conversation had changed. It was about my report card and then it was about me and then it was all the old bitterness.

I didn't say a word. No sense in reminding her that I didn't ask to be born. One word from me and I knew her temper would boil over, and there was no telling what she would do then. Everyone thought she was a wonderful teacher, but I drove her to the brink.

She wouldn't let go. "I'll learn, I promise," I choked out because I knew that's what I had to say.

Slowly, her grip loosened. "I'll hold you to that. I've had enough. You need to be able to read the prescription bottles and the instructions from the doctors and to read her those silly romance stories when Mother's eyes are too tired. I'll look into getting you a special tutor, even if it means taking the bus to Grand Falls every Saturday. I'm leaving and you're the one who has to stay. It's your turn. It's only fair."

A part of me wanted to take the gold cross that Lady had worn all her life, which Dad had given to me on the day she was buried, and fling it in her face. Maybe Dad should have given the cross to Louise since I got the money, but he didn't. Truly, I thought, if she wanted it that bad, she should have it. If it kept her here, it was worth giving it to her. But then I touched it and felt the warm metal in my hand. No, I thought, she'd lost her temper, but this time I wouldn't lose mine. The cross kept me close to Lady, and

holding the cross wrapped in my fist reminded me that I didn't
want to end up mean and contrary, sour and pinched, like Louise.

THERE WAS A SONG on the radio in those days about a hick town
that had only one gas station and one movie theatre. Well, I would
have been thrilled to have either. There was nothing in
Riverbank—no movies, no restaurants, not even a french fry
shack, nowhere to buy clothes. All the teenagers couldn't wait to
bust out of the utter boredom of spending evenings watching one
of two channels on TV or walking up and down the road, cruising
they called it: dressing up so that people (I mean boys seeing girls
and girls seeing boys) could get a look at the latest sweaters, boots
and hats that had come from the catalogues and from shopping
trips in Grand Falls, Gander and St. John's. It used to be that
people would get together in their homes for a singalong, but that
was dying out; it was so much easier now to turn on the stereo and
play records. At Christmastime there used to be mummering,
where men and women dressed in old clothes and went door to
door getting people to guess who they were. Dad said it was great
fun. If I wanted to be mean I'd say that gossip and waiting for
welfare money and watching who was spending their money on
beer were the favourite pastimes nowadays. Some of the kids got
drunk on Saturday nights on moonshine made from potato skins,
and I'd overheard some of them talking about drugs that made the
boredom go away.

In truth, the few people who decided to settle in our town of
three hundred or so souls seemed to be happy enough; they liked
being apart. The people the age of my parents actually preferred

this isolated life, no bones about it. Many of them would vote against a bridge across the river if a petition went around, as the government was promising for the next election.

St. Albert's was a lot better for people who liked to be social. One or two of our young people moved to St. Albert's every year either to get married or to work on the coastal steamers or at the hydro plant. There were dances at the Legion, a couple of general stores, and Mac's Place, a little lean-to on the back of Mac MacDonald's house where you could get a grilled hamburger and french fries.

There was still seasonal work to be had down our way—inshore fishing for cod, guiding for rich Americans who wanted a photograph of themselves with a ten-pound salmon caught in the river or moose antlers to take back home, working in the camps as cooks and cleaners, and fixing the gravel roads every summer. There was enough work around in the summer for most folks to qualify for unemployment cheques in the winter. Every so often a couple of the younger guys went to Grand Falls to work in the paper mill, and at first they'd come home on weekends loaded with money. They were very popular for a while, but then even that got boring, and soon enough they stopped coming home because there was nowhere to spend their pocketfuls of cash. Several of the family men, like my dad, went far away for permanent jobs, their families unwilling to give up on our way of life or a home that had been in the family for generations.

The boredom seemed to be especially bad for girls, who—this was 1971, remember—were still meant to grow up to keep house and have babies. Babies *after* you were married, not before, that is.

I'd seen on TV that some women were doctors and lawyers, but those lofty careers were not for our kind. Even Louise, a perfectly good principal who kept an easy discipline in the school and who sent more kids to the high school in St. Albert's than ever before, was seen as something of a vague failure because she hadn't bagged a man—the kind of man who would allow her to continue teaching, mind you.

My favourite dream was of riding out of this place in a powerful white speedboat. There was no prince, just me, tearing across the water, cresting the waves, free.

I got to visiting Lady's grave more and more. It gave me comfort to know I could still share my goals with someone, even if she couldn't hear me. It was where I did my heavy thinking. The cemetery up on the hill was cold, but I hardly noticed or cared. I put on a couple of layers of sweaters, borrowed Dad's big oiled sea jacket off the hook in the back porch and huddled in it beside Lady's new granite tombstone, which Dad had sent down from Nova Scotia. I would stay there, still and silent, until Bush whimpered and nipped at my heels to get me moving.

While I sat beside her grave, curled up in my dad's old coat, I would think of all the times I had run to Lady. There were cuts and bruises that needed boo-boo kisses, hair that needed untangling, jeans that needed patches, molasses bread that needed to be eaten, gloves that needed matching, glasses that constantly needed to be taped back together and scraps from her table that needed to be saved for Bush.

It had been me and Lady for as long as I could remember. No matter how many ugly report cards I brought home, she gently urged me to try again, and again, and again. I could so easily have never gone to school—like my friend Mildred. Everyone knew that she was truant, but no one reported her to the school board. If she had been forced to go to school, the whole Spence family would have fallen apart. I went to school when I did because Lady believed that one day I would catch on. Now there was no Lady and it was really, really hard.

THEN THE MOST absolutely amazing thing happened. But as good as it was, it didn't change my mind about quitting school and getting a job come June. In fact, it made it easier to make real plans.

It just so happened that we had a spelling test one Friday. Louise got wind of it and forced me to sit at the kitchen table to study for it. I was pretty good at looking like I was all ears and eyes while my mind drifted off to the barrens for a bit of fishing, swimming or tracking partridges. Even with Beryl prodding me and starting to help me a bit after school, and me needing to learn, it all seemed hopeless. Of course, I didn't learn a single word that evening, and of course I got a zero on the test like I always did. Usually I didn't even bother to take the silly tests; I'd slip out of the classroom while everyone else cleared their desks. This time I was feeling quite contrary, so I hung around to write some childish squiggles on the test sheet. I wanted to show Louise once and for all just how impossible things were with me and school. And a small part of me wanted to see for myself just how bad I was.

She was livid when I came home from school on Monday with the test and a big fat zero in black marker across the top.

"I saw you study myself, you had the book open for at least two hours. How could you not have learned anything at all?" she ragged at me. I shrugged my shoulders, and that sent her around the loony bend.

She grabbed me and pushed me onto a kitchen chair. Now, this wasn't an easy thing to do, because while we were the same height, I had a good thirty pounds on her. But her anger gave her a furious strength.

"You're going back tomorrow and rewriting that test, and you're going to pass. Do you hear me? I'm tired of you getting away with being as lazy as a dog. You're refusing to do well— you've always been stubborn. But now, young lady, it's gone too far. You'll never finish high school with zeros."

Finish high school! Was she totally nuts? I asked myself. Here I was trying to figure out how to learn enough to get by and here was Louise thinking I was going to graduate, go all the way to grade eleven. I bet she had plans to send me to university! Totally delusional, she was.

I couldn't ignore her. She was hissing words through clamped teeth and stamping her feet as she circled me.

"What's going on out there?" Mother called down the hall.

Louise hurled me a furious look. "Oh, nothing, Mother. Issy is studying and I'm helping her."

"Please keep it down, I'm trying to watch *The Saint*." Mother hated to be disturbed when her spy shows were on.

It wasn't like we hadn't done this a hundred times before. Louise sincerely believed that I was lazy and that if she shouted things at me long enough and loud enough, I would get them.

It wasn't that I wasn't trying. I really *wanted* to read. But no matter how hard I looked, those things called words were just a jumble of black smudges on the page. Each one looked slightly different, but too many were alike for me to pick among them to identify what they were. I couldn't believe that everyone else could see words in the nasty little marks. And it didn't matter if I had my glasses on or if I took them off—it was all the same. Sometimes, if I tilted my glasses just the right way, I could make out some letters, but I didn't know how to string them together or what letters made up what words.

Then it happened. Louise and I were going at it tooth and nail. She was close to losing her cool entirely, and she had already run through every demented thing she could call me without swearing at me or taking God's name in vain. And I've got to hand it to her, not once did she call me stupid. Not this time.

Louise decided that a pass wouldn't be good enough, that I was going to go back and get a hundred percent. She was in a rage about it. We went over the twenty words dozens of times. At one point I had them all memorized. She called out the words, I sang them back to her, every last one of them, the way I had learned them.

She was very, very pleased. She smiled, and I was happy too. I had finally achieved what all the other kids had done, and it only took four hours of study. If it meant I would have to work ten times harder than everyone else, I vowed to myself that I would.

Then Louise said, "One last time, okay?" And I stupidly said, "Fine." She called them out again, I spelled them back to her. Then she threw the spelling book across the room.

"You had them memorized!" she yelled so loud I jumped an inch off my chair. Well, yes, of course. It turned out she had changed the order of the words, but I had stuck to the list the way I had learned it by heart.

It was midnight and we had to start over. I was mad for being found out, but she was even madder.

"This time we are going to learn each word separately," she forced out from between very tight lips. Then she ripped a whole page out of my scribbler, wrapped her fingers tightly around a short pencil, and crushed out two words, *telephone* and *candidate*, big enough to fill the whole page.

"You're not going to bed tonight until you have these two words," she spit out and then moved to the stove to make herself a cup of tea.

Before she had taken three steps, I said, "I have them."

"Don't be silly. I'm getting my tea, and don't waste my time."

"I really do! The writing is so big that I see all the letters. I know them, honest."

Louise let out a big sigh and turned back to the table. She asked me the words and I spelled them for her. Didn't matter which one she said first or second. She looked at me like I was a dead horse that had got up and kicked her. "Can you manage another two tonight?"

I said sure, why not go for the jackpot. Another two, and the same thing happened—I knew the words instantly. By this time Louise had forgotten about her tea. We tried another two. She mixed up all eight. I got them all flawlessly. The next two I got almost as fast as she could write them out. By this time Louise had to sit down and catch her breath.

"What's happened, what's different?" she asked, with just a trace of a tremor in her voice.

That was easy for me to answer. "I can see the letters. I can see that putting a string of letters together makes a word. I can see that if you say the letters in order, you get a word. When you write them big like that, I can see how the letters are different, they're not all black smudges."

There was a huge silence in the room. Finally Louise was able to speak.

"You mean all these years all you ever saw was black smudges on a page? Oh my goodness, Isabelle, I never believed you when you said that. Can you write the letters, do you think?"

I shook my head. I hadn't written any alphabet letters since grade two and I'd forgotten how it was done. The teachers had ignored my blank test papers and no homework for years and years.

It was hard to take it in, even harder for Louise. She came closer and stood beside me, gripping the back of my chair, first with a look of thunder flittering across her face, then surprise and finally sadness.

"Oh, Issy, it's all my fault. All these years we've treated you like a … well … a moron. There, I've said it, though I always knew you weren't. You're not backward at all—it's your eyes! I can't even imagine what it must have been like for you growing up. Why didn't I notice?"

"Louise, it wasn't your fault. I was the one who wouldn't read the eye chart."

"It *is* my fault. I won't let you say that it wasn't. I never looked beyond the obvious. I knew you could be smart enough when it suited you. I never put two and two together. All these years, Issy, my God!"

"No, Louise, it was me. You're not to blame at all. Please don't worry about it," I begged as I saw the anguish on her face.

But she wouldn't let up. "Issy, you wouldn't have known the difference. Whatever you see is normal to you. It's the only world you know. None of us asked you about it. None of us encouraged you to tell us if you had a problem. We just told you over and over that it was easy to learn and that you were being stubborn. I feel awful."

I had never seen my sister so contrite. She looked softer somehow. She looked like she needed a hug, and I was so happy I almost felt like giving her one. Almost. But a lot of hard years got in the way. Instead, she awkwardly patted my shoulder and I hesitantly reached back to touch her hand, and our touch was a mere flutter of fingertips.

"I'll help you, Issy, I promise. The first thing we're going to do is to get your eyes checked and get you new glasses that work. Now off to bed. It's been a big night for you."

And with that, I floated off to the bedroom.

As I lay in the dark, I felt excitement mingled with what could only be pain. Despite what I had said to Louise, she—and even Lady—had not helped where I had needed it the most. I pounded my head on the bed as I remembered the Christmas when Lady gave up on me and my reading. Lady had read the story of *The Ugly Duckling* to me over and over, and sometimes I read it to her.

It was a story I loved, the little duck getting mixed up with the wrong family but everything turning out okay when they discovered she was a swan, not a duck at all. Oh, how I wished that were me. Then, for Christmas when I was eight, Lady got me a new version of the story with prettier pictures. It was then she discovered I had the story memorized. I saw the disappointment flicker across her face when she realized I couldn't read a word and that's when I flung the book across the room and yelled that I was too old for such a silly, childish story anyway. Lady never asked me to read again, and I never again opened a book in her house.

I had a pillowful of dreams that night: Lady was wheeling a cartload of books toward me and a swan was sitting on top of the wagon flapping its wings. A teacher handed me a report card and golden stars spilled out onto the floor for everyone to see. My mother tied angel wings across my shoulders and gently pushed me off a cliff so I could fly.

In the morning when I awoke, the sun seemed brighter, the air lighter—the darkness in my world had gone away. Oh, I knew I still had tough times ahead, but somehow I also knew I would get through them.

I bounced out of bed and gave Bush a great big rough dog hug. My life had changed forever; there would be no looking back.

CHAPTER SIX

Streel: untidy, dirty person, esp. a woman

When Mother was young and beautiful, Louise told me once, her social life was a whirl of Hollywood films, West End theatre, dancing, late night dinner parties and shopping weekends in Paris, Brussels and Berlin. Then a handsome navy guy whisked her more than two thousand miles away and her life was never the same again. The story didn't have a happy ending. She came with her sailor to Newfoundland and she could not, or would not, adapt. She treated the people she met as colonials and wrapped herself in her upper-class Englishness. She hated the rocks, the hills, the short summer, the long winter, the neighbours who talked very oddly indeed, the wooden houses, the lack of green vegetables and fresh fruit, the gaudy colours, the closeness to the water, the distance from England, the tea—whatever. I felt she hung on because Gander International Airport, the crossroads of the world, was just a hundred and fifty miles up a gravel road and she had this vision of herself flying back to her whirlwind of a British life. Sometimes she and Louise would talk for hours about the "old country."

I could never prove it, but I strongly suspected that Mother managed to arrange "an attack" whenever things weren't going her way. I will accept that her first one, the one that happened shortly after I was born, was genuine. And I accept she was weak for a few months after that. But once Louise was home looking after me, I can see how she might just have found it easier to stay in bed. She let it slip one time that back in England she had a great-aunt who went to bed when she was forty and never left it again. "Great-aunt Mary had three daughters," Mother gloated, "and they never married so they could take care of their mother." Well, that was back in the 1920s; the same stunt wasn't going to work in the 1970s. Except, of course, it *was* working. Louise was already a spinster, and I had to be careful not to be sucked in by the tidal wave of Mother's needs.

Mother had an episode the time Dad got her the tray instead of the charm she wanted. She had another one a few years back when Louise's friend Maisy asked her to come stay with her over in St. Albert's for a week. That trip was cancelled. She was on the brink of yet another attack when Maisy was getting married and it looked like Louise, as maid of honour, might have to stay over across the harbour for the one night because it would be too late and cold to cross the river in her chiffon dress. But the pains went away when Louise arranged for the Petersons to bring her home as soon as the wedding supper was finished at the Legion.

Mother used to have little twinges near her heart whenever Dad was getting ready to go back to work. He fixed her wagon by coming home less and less, and when he did, he didn't unpack but lived out of his suitcase. When he was ready to leave, he would just appear in the kitchen with his bag in his hand. Louise and I knew what he was up to and we'd say our goodbyes in low voices that wouldn't carry down the hall.

She had another attack the morning after the amazing night I was able to turn smudges into words. When I got up that day, Louise, smiling as wide as a Cheshire cat, almost prettily in fact, had cooked me a full Newfie breakfast of eggs, bacon, fried bread and pork, beans and scalding hot tea. Her arm touched my shoulder as she brought my plate to the table and put it in front of me with a flourish. I liked the touch, it was brief but very sisterly, or at least how I imagined sisterly to be.

I was scoffing down the last of my breakfast feast when there was a crash in Mother's bedroom. Louise froze, her hand in mid-air as it picked up her teacup. "I can't believe it," she said, "the first morning ever I didn't bring her tea in at seven-thirty." She looked at me. "I wanted this to be a special morning for you." Then, in an instant, the cup was on its saucer and Louise was racing down the hall.

Louise waved me off, told me to go to school, as she phoned the doctor. At lunchtime I went home to find Mother still quite ill, with Louise and the doctor scurrying around with ice packs and Aspirin.

Mother did look rather pale against the white sheets, and her breathing was shallow and she moaned through the night. Louise was there to give her sips of water and to feed her beef broth and little fingers of toast. On the second day of the "attack," Dr. David pronounced that she had a very bad case of the flu that was making the rounds, and that he had better find a place to sleep on our side of the river because all this going back and forth across the icy water was killing him. If Mother had been feeling better, you can bet she would have convinced him that no way on earth did she have the flu, but that her heart was giving out on her and death was but a breath away.

Louise ordered me to clean and dust the bedroom Dad used when he came home, and the doctor moved in. Another dozen people had the flu in a serious way and he hardly turned down the sheets for the first forty-eight hours.

Then the crisis was over. Oh, Mother was still moaning and needed care, but the doctor said she was as comfortable at night as medicine could make her, and he ordered Louise to get some rest herself. Mother was so annoyed, she got up to see what was going on, forgetting that she was supposed to be quite ill.

I woke up on Thursday morning to the smell of raisin scones and bacon and eggs. I drifted toward the kitchen expecting to see Louise making up the fancy tray. But no, she was setting the table.

"Good morning, Issy. Could you finish setting the table, please?"

I took my time stretching so I could figure out what was going on. We weren't in the habit of saying good morning to each other, and a "please" wasn't part of our daily ritual either. I craned my neck around the corner.

Ah, the good doctor was sitting at the end of the table working on some papers and Louise was at the stove wearing a pretty apron, and her long golden hair, usually tied up in a neat but severe bun, was shimmering in waves down her back.

Hmmm, I thought, I could tell her to piss off, like normal, or I could meekly set the table and continue with this picture of domestic bliss.

Louise shot me a look that said "Don't you dare," so I set the table just like I'd seen them do it on an old TV show, *Leave It to Beaver*. As I folded the last linen napkin from Mother's special supply, the timer went off for the scones and Louise was breaking eggs into the frying pan.

"Sit in your usual place, Issy, and I'll bring you breakfast," Louise said. I looked at her for a hint as to what my "usual place" would be, but she had her back turned to me. I grabbed the chair nearest me and plunked myself down. Two cooked breakfasts in under a week, it was almost too much. Louise put a plate with four slices of bacon, two eggs, sunny side up, and two hot scones in front of me, and I picked up my fork and was about to dig in when I heard someone say, "Hummmm."

It was Louise, and her eyebrows were practically on the ceiling. Oh yes, I remembered, I was supposed to wait until she sat down. I'd seen that on TV too. She whipped off her apron, the doctor managed to lean across to pull out her chair, and we became the image of a happy family.

It was a quiet meal. The doctor was reading his notes, I had nothing to say, and, bless Louise, she was not a jabber-mouth. We listened to the news on the radio: the U.S. was talking again of withdrawing all troops from Vietnam and there were rumours that Princess Margaret was heading for a divorce. There was a state of emergency in St. John's because of a snow-storm, and our prime minister, Mr. Trudeau, was in India. I had no trouble remembering all the ins and outs of royalty and governments.

I got up to bring my plate to the sink and started filling the dish basin with water, but Louise said no, she would do that. "Go get ready for school."

Just as I was leaving and Louise was cleaning up and the doctor was putting things in his bag to start his rounds, Mother called from her bedroom in a whispery voice, "Do I smell bacon and scones? Louise, I'm feeling a lot better this morning. Bring me a tray."

That's when the doctor came to life. Like I said, he had no trouble talking if it was anything to do with medicine or a patient. "I'll deal with your mother, Miss Heffernan. Make her some toast, no butter. I've looked at her case thoroughly over the past couple of months. It's the flu right now, but she does have a stressed heart. It would be a lot less stressed if she were to lose fifty pounds. The diet starts today. I've made up a list of things she can eat and I'll be monitoring very closely. I'll break the news to her, you make the toast."

A perfect time to dash out the door. I headed off to school all spruced up, nothing like the streel I usually was. I'd even had time to run a comb through my tangles. I soon realized I wasn't as agitated as I was most mornings. I wasn't hungry, and I was smiling at the idea of Mother going on a diet. Young Rosalie Peterson caught up to me and wanted to know what I was so happy about. Happy? Me? A strange concept indeed.

I LIKED TO WATCH HOCKEY on TV, especially *Hockey Night in Canada* on Saturday nights. My favourite player was Frank

Mahovlich and I also liked to watch Gordie Howe and Bobby Hull. In February, Eddie Shack, as in "clear the track, here comes Shack," got a hat trick, three goals in one game, and everyone went hockey nuts. It took our minds off the other dreary news: The FLQ, a group that wanted a quick separation of Quebec from Canada, had kidnapped a politician and a diplomat in the fall, Pierre Laporte and James Cross. They killed Laporte and released Cross after they bargained for a flight to Cuba. But some other members of the group were arrested in December, and now their trials were all over the TV and radio.

When Wish dropped by yet again, he wanted to talk about hockey, thank goodness, because what was going on in Quebec was just too bleak. "The Toronto Maple Leafs are an embarrassment. The way they're going, they'll never win the Stanley Cup again. Serves them right for trading Tim Horton." He knew that would make me mad because, as bad as the Leafs were, the honourable thing to do was to stand by them. That's what fans did.

It was the Saturday after the doctor started my mother on her diet. Louise had gone up to the school to catch up on lesson plans, because she had missed a week of teaching. I was "babysitting," or guarding Mother, like I had never done before. The doctor said that if she lost fifty pounds, she would feel a lot better. If she started feeling better, there was a chance she wouldn't need a handmaid. I was determined to do my part, so I wouldn't have to feel so guilty about leaving Louise behind.

Louise had given Mother her broth and crackers for supper before leaving, and my job was to make sure that Mother didn't slip down to the kitchen and, if she did, to tell Louise what she had eaten. We were pretty serious about this diet.

Wish had walked in just before nine-thirty. I was curled up in the one comfortable chair in the room, an old cracked-leather wing chair that Dad had hauled home from an antique store on the mainland and fixed up on one of his trips.

Wish said hello as he sat down and turned on the TV. I poked my nose up from the blanket I had wrapped around me. I still wasn't used to having him around, and certainly not used to having someone walk into our house and sit down like they owned the place. I could only guess this was the way it was done in other homes because Wish looked so comfortable doing it.

He opened a paper bag he was carrying under his arm. "Want a Coke?" I shook my head. He peered deep into the bag again. "How about potato chips—or a Cherry Blossom?"

I had to hide a smile then, because only Wish knew that Cherry Blossoms were my favourite candy bar. He remembered after six years away.

"Come on, don't be a sulk, I got it for you. You know I hate the gooey things," he said as he got up from the chesterfield, took a step across the room and put the little yellow box with the red cherries on the arm of my chair.

Just as he sat down, our side door opened again and Beryl Peterson walked in. Now that was a surprise. Beryl had been friendly enough at school since the accident, and while I'd let her help me a couple of times up at the school, that had dropped off again when Mother got sick. She, the most popular girl in Riverbank, had never been inside the door of my home and now she was acting like we were pals. I could only think she was trying to impress Wish.

"Hi Wish, hi Issy. I was hoping you'd be watching the game," she said as she took off her heavy winter pea jacket and flopped onto the couch beside Wish—not too close, mind you, a safe, friendly distance. She tugged at her short skirt until it covered at least six inches of her thighs. She too had a paper bag under her arm, and a very big purse. She patted her handbag and looked toward me. "I've got this weekend's homework here if you want to get a start on it between periods. I know you had a bad week with your mother getting sick again and we started some new stuff in math and in English." I pretty well ignored this little speech.

Since I had figured out almost a week ago that words were within my reach, I was eager to see what I could do. In fact, I wanted to stand on the government wharf and scream my good news up and down the river and across the harbour. Now, though, I snuggled down into my blanket. No way on earth was I going to let Beryl open a book in front of Wish. I didn't mind them using me to meet, but he would have to leave before I did any homework.

Beryl reached into her paper bag. "Want a Coke?"

Well, I had to smile. Two Cokes in one night. I only ever had Coke when Louise brought a bottle home from the store to make Coke floats on Sunday evenings. She would split the Coke, carefully measuring out four ounces for each of us, and add one scoop of vanilla ice cream. Beryl saw the smile and took it as a yes. Wish opened the bottle with his penknife and Beryl handed it to me with her eyes on the game.

I silently opened the Cherry Blossom and ate that too; it seemed silly to not eat it when Wish had gone to special trouble to get it. I knew for certain that the Petersons did not sell Cherry Blossoms, so he must have got it in a shop around the bay.

A half-hour into the game, Wish's hands reached for his pack of cigarettes. Just the thought of anyone smoking within a hundred yards of Mother got me rattled.

"No, Wish, you can't smoke in here. It hurts my mother's chest," I said in not much more than a whisper. Plus, it would let her know someone was visiting. The less Mother knew, the better.

That's when Beryl punched him on the arm. "You shouldn't smoke anyway. You're killing yourself, don't you hear what doctors say about smoking?"

Wish's hand dropped back to his side and he blushed a faint pink. "I'm sorry. I should know better. My aunt always said the same thing and wouldn't let me smoke in her house in Toronto."

Her house. I heard that. He didn't say "home" or even "our house." Somehow the young man on the couch disappeared in front of my eyes and I saw a young boy left all alone in the world. I hated to see hurt children. I struggled out of my blanket.

"Wish," I said, and fought to find words, "I still like to play hockey, you know. The ice is good. Can we play tomorrow in your cove?" It was the least I could do for my old friend.

"I love hockey too," chimed in Beryl. "What time?"

What gall! It never crossed her mind that she wouldn't be welcome.

"How about two tomorrow afternoon? Would that be okay, Issy? I'd love a good game of hockey," he said with a warm smile crinkling the corners of his eyes. It was settled.

"What's going on out there? Is that Louise talking?" Beryl and Wish knew I had to go tend to Mother, and the Leafs were losing yet again, so they got up to leave, very quietly.

"I'll come by on Monday to help you with your homework," whispered Beryl at the door. And she was true to her word.

I HAD LONG AGO OUTGROWN the skimpy second-hand hockey equipment that I had as a child, so I only had to grab my old, black, boy's skates from the back porch before heading down to Sweetapple Cove. It was the tiniest of inlets, just big enough to be the front yard of one house at the end of Sweetapple Lane. In the summer the Sweetapples had their own private beach on their doorstep, and in the winter they had a skating rink. The Sweetapples had built the house facing the little beach at the beginning of the century, about the same time as the Heffernans arrived in Riverbank, though both families came after the Joes and the Jeddores, who were from a long line of Micmac Indians. With his grandfather having only one child, Wish's father, and Wish off in Toronto, the Sweetapples would be disappearing in these parts. I wondered for a moment if this was weighing on Wish's mind.

Wish was already on the ice, wearing a helmet and knee pads over grey, fleece-lined pants. There was an extra hockey stick and a battered helmet set up against a tree on the shore. I was always breaking my hockey stick when I was a youngster, and Wish had guessed rightly that I wouldn't have one. The helmet was a good, snug fit.

Beryl came tramping through the snow behind me. She'd taken a shortcut along the river and was already working up a sweat. She had knee pads and a helmet slung over her shoulder, tied to her hockey stick and skates.

"We got ourselves a beautiful day," she said as she found a fallen tree trunk to sit on to tie up her skates.

It was cold, but the sun was shining, so I hung my parka on a tree branch. Wish was making goalposts out of bits of wood he found along the shore and was measuring off the distance for a blue line.

The idea was to get the puck in the "net." Each of us would take a turn starting at the blue line while the other two tried to stop you. No hitting, no slashing, no hooking. Wish had taught me to play fair and square.

I started off shaky. It was clear that Wish and Beryl had kept up their skills. I remembered there was talk that if the high school in St. Albert's would let girls on the hockey team, Beryl would be their first choice. Of course, we knew that wasn't going to happen.

The three of us were well matched in size and tenacity, though I was heavier than Beryl. Soon the things I'd learned as a kid came back to me and it wasn't so easy for either of them to scoop the puck from me. My biggest problem was that, with all the sweating, my glasses kept fogging up.

Now, Sweetapple Cove was almost invisible when I was a kid. It's why Wish and I used to play there. But I'd forgotten that, in the six years since he'd left, three families had built houses farther up in the hills that rose behind Riverbank. The cove was in clear view of these houses. Each family had two or three boys, and it wasn't long before six of them showed up on the shore, hockey sticks in hand. And Beryl's brothers must have seen her leave, because they were stumbling along the river path with two friends, all carrying pads and sticks.

I wanted to stamp my foot and yell at them all to go away. It was the first time in a long while that I was having fun, and they were going to spoil it all for me. These boys were the tough kids, the ones who bullied the little ones in the school playground. Even Beryl's brothers were snotty little boys.

Wish and Beryl took one last shot on the net and skated toward the kids. "The ice is great, it's really fast today. Come on, get your skates on and show us what you can do," said Wish.

Don't they know that's not the way to get rid of people? I thought.

The boys were pretty good, a lot better than I was at their age. They were going across the bay to the new ice rink for proper hockey lessons and they played on peewee teams. There was no holding them back once they were on the ice.

Wish shrugged his shoulders toward me, grinned, and asked if I wanted to be part of the toss to choose teams. I shrugged my shoulders too, meaning what the heck, and I was the second one picked to play with the Bandits, the name the boys on the blue team had chosen for themselves. I knew they wanted me for my size, but it was still pretty flattering. I had never been picked by anyone for any team before.

It was a lot more fun than I'd expected it to be; the boys played serious hockey and expected me to keep up my end. The guy they chose as captain, young Arnie McDonald, from grade six, kept barking out the orders and was pretty fair about giving players chances to score a goal and chances to catch a breath.

The Bandits won, four to three. It was amazing. I was the goalie, and Arnie told everyone it was that last save that did it for our team. Beryl was in the other net and Wish was the referee.

We had to quit because it was getting so dark we couldn't see the puck. I was skating back to shore when I turned and saw all the players shaking hands in a snake line. I didn't know what to do and Wish skated toward me.

"Hey, Issy, stay right there, we're coming to you." And that's what the two teams did, they skated over to me and lined up again and shook hands. "Great game, Issy, great game," they said.

The boys melted into the darkness. "Why don't you two come to my house for hot chocolate? You need to cool down before you walk home or you'll get really cold," said Wish.

It made sense. I could already feel my temperature going down, the sweat was freezing in my hair, and my back was chilled to the bone.

But I hesitated. Wish's grandfather was known to be cranky, and no one had seen him smile since his son had died and Wish had been hauled off to Toronto. And Wish's great-aunt Effie had hinted at a fight between the Heffernans and the Sweetapples.

"Granddad will likely be asleep," said Wish.

"Then I'm in," said Beryl.

I nodded. What the heck, I thought, Wish was making a habit of coming to my house; it was time I found out how he was making out living with his grandfather.

I was in for a surprise.

I KNEW WISH'S GRANDFATHER only from afar. He used to be a quiet man who minded his own business. He had been the fisheries officer for years and had spent a good deal of time up on the salmon rivers on his own, but he had retired when I was a child. He had also been an artillery captain in World War I, so he had to be at least seventy-five years old. Some people still called him Captain. The last time I had seen him up close was at Lady's funeral. I noticed him then because, when everyone had left the cemetery, I looked back up the hill and, through my tears, saw him at the foot of her grave with his hands crossed, head down, grey curls blowing in the wind, not seeming to notice the cold.

It didn't make sense to me because, in all my years of spending time with Lady, I'd never seen them talk to each other. And thinking about it, it was strange that the two oldest people in Riverbank, the only two left who had gone overseas for the first war, never visited back and forth. I wondered if the gulf between them was the difference between their war experiences: Lady had spent her war years in a government office in London and then several months in Paris in 1919 as a secretary at a conference, while the Captain had been in the trenches in France. Sometimes when I asked about those years, Lady would quote a writer she liked, Charles Dickens. Looking into the distance, she'd say simply, "They were the best of times; they were the worst of times." We studied World War I in our history class and the teacher told us about the thousands and thousands of men killed at the Battle of the Somme and at Vimy Ridge, and how almost an entire regiment of Newfoundlanders was wiped out at a small place called Beaumont-Hamel in France. That's when I came to have an inkling of what she was talking about.

Like I said, since Wish's dad and mom died, the least little thing would set his grandfather off. He'd shout at the children for playing too close to the shore or he'd rant and rave about the weather or how drugs and alcohol were the ruin of the young generation. If I ever saw him coming toward me, I'd turn and go the opposite way, as did most people in Riverbank.

When we came in through the kitchen, Mr. Sweetapple was asleep in his rocking chair with a newspaper spread across his chest. Wish put his finger to his lips and pointed toward the living room. I was expecting an old-fashioned parlour, but it wasn't a dreary, dark room at all; instead it was bright and comfortable, with a modern green chesterfield, matching drapes and rug, and a big TV. Pictures of Wish as a baby and of his mom and dad were on top of the TV, all neatly framed in dark wood. There was a photo of Wish's dad when he graduated from high school, and one of Wish's grandmother, a small, thin woman who looked very sad. I remembered then that she died of a bad heart about a year after Wish's parents were killed. The memory came back like a kick in the head, because I had thought that Wish would surely come back for his grandmother's funeral. He didn't. The lawyer and his wife sent a massive bouquet of white lillies specially flown in from Halifax in the dead of winter.

Beryl was going on about what a great game we'd had and how she hadn't had a good workout like that since last Christmas. There was never a problem with embarrassing silences wherever Beryl was. Wish came in with the hot chocolate on a tray and made room for it on the low coffee table.

"I made it with fresh milk, not that Carnation stuff, and lots of sugar," Wish said as he sat down. We had barely taken a few sips when there was a rustle from the kitchen. "Granddad is just waking up," Wish explained as he waved his hand toward the noise.

Beryl knew right away that this was some coded message. "We won't keep you then, Wish. You must have to help get supper ready." She drank down her chocolate in noisy slurps before I was halfway through mine, and then she was lifting me up by the elbows. "Time to go, Issy. Don't get comfortable. Put your sweater and your coat on, don't want to feel cold." Bossy or what.

Mr. Sweetapple was still sitting in his rocking chair, looking a little dazed, as we came back through the kitchen. I wanted more than anything to sneak past him, not to get him upset.

"Who is that?" he asked as he reached for his glasses.

Wish knew his manners. "Granddad, this here is Beryl Peterson and the other one is Issy. We were playing hockey and I got them some hot chocolate. I would have asked you, but you were asleep." He said "Issy" like "Well, you know Issy, of course."

"You know that whatever is here is yours, boy. You don't have to ask. I know the Petersons. Buy all my groceries at your store. Tell your father to get proper tea in, not those silly bags. What is your last name, child?" he barked out as he looked up at me with watery blue eyes from his chair.

"She's a Heffernan, Granddad, Lady Heffernan's grand-niece. Her mom and dad are Nobe and Agnes, you know, the one who came here from England."

Mr. Sweetapple sat bolt upright when he heard my name and lineage. "What's a Heffernan doing in my house? They're nothing but trouble, and the women are hussies," he all but shouted.

Wish and Beryl and I, we didn't know what to do or what to say. Family feuds were common enough, with whole families not talking to each other for generations because someone got a fishing licence and someone else didn't, or a net was destroyed, or a piece of land that was promised to be fertile turned out to be only rocks. We all looked at each other, confirming with our eyes that none of us knew anything about a fight between our families, certainly nothing about Heffernan women who were hussies. Nothing had been said those two years when Wish and I were kids and together all the time. Maybe his granddad was remembering something from long ago. Mrs. John did that sometimes.

Mr. Sweetapple started to get up from his chair and he had a thundering look on his face. Then he took a coughing fit.

"I'll get you some water, Granddad. Sit down."

Beryl and I decided it was a good time to bolt out the door. And we did.

THE NEXT DAY at school was very odd. I sat alone during the first recess and then again at dinner, because Beryl had a library meeting and didn't come around to bother me. In truth, I was starting to think she wasn't much of a bother anymore. At the second recess, in the afternoon, I was pushing some of the little ones on the swings when I noticed that the bully boys were standing around the chain-link fence of the playground.

"Hey, Issy, come here. I want to talk to you," one of them shouted.

I tightened my stomach and pulled my jacket closer around me, and my fists went into a ball. If one of them so much as touched a single hair on any of the little ones, I was ready to split open their heads.

"Come on, Issy, it's important."

I didn't move. I heard the playground gate open and the little ones stopped playing and froze. It was big tough Arnie.

"Look, Issy, we're hoping the ice will stay good tomorrow, and we're going to ask the teachers if we can have a long dinner break so we can get a game of hockey in. We're wondering if you can play goal again."

That was the very last thing I expected. I gulped, unclenched my fists and stared at him. Slowly I nodded.

"That's great, Issy. The Peterson boys are asking their sister, too, so we'll be evenly matched. Here, let me push one of these kids. I bet I can push higher than you can."

Later, Beryl came by the house like she had promised. "I hear we're both goalies again tomorrow," she said as she set down a pile of books.

Louise was in with Mother, trying to cajole her into eating canned fruit. She was definitely over the flu, because all she talked about now was how hungry she was all the time.

Dr. David had moved back to the apartment above his clinic across the river, but he had taken Mother and her diet on as a personal crusade. He'd left a number of low-calorie recipes for Louise to try, and as I watched Louise, I was learning them too. Mother wasn't going to like getting one skinned chicken breast with tinned green peas on the side for supper, but that was her meal a couple of evenings a week. The doctor said it would be better if she had a green salad, but a head of lettuce was almost impossible to buy in winter. Her only sweets were to be marshmallow squares, and we had orders to put a sugar substitute in the dozen cups of tea she had every day. No more deep-fried fish or chicken or homemade fried doughnuts rolled in sugar for Mother—or for any of us, for that matter.

"We've put this off for two weeks, but it's time to get started or there just won't be time to catch up," Beryl said. "Come on, find a pen and let's do math first."

That's when I had to decide if I trusted Beryl. Could she really help me? I wondered.

I moved to the kitchen table and flopped into a chair. She pushed the book toward me. "See, the first problem is about families and hats. You have to get each of your thirteen brothers and sisters a cowboy hat to wear to the silly family picnic. If each hat costs eight dollars, how many hours are you going to have to work at four dollars an hour to pay for those hats?"

I thought about it for a minute and said, "Twenty-six."

"Wow," she said, unable to cover her surprise. "Write the answer down here." She handed me a sheet of paper. Now I could write my numbers, and after squishing my glasses so I could see the page I carefully wrote a two and a six. "You read the next problem for me since you're so smart," Beryl said.

I broke out into a sweat. I looked and looked at the page, but I couldn't read a thing. I took my glasses off and put them back on and fiddled with them up and down my nose. I twisted my head and I could see letters and words, but none that I recognized from my spelling test.

"Ah," said Beryl, "it all goes back to reading, doesn't it." She looked at me with understanding in her eyes and I wanted to hug her to pieces.

I struggled to find my voice. "I can see the words if you make them really big. Louise and I discovered this just a week or so ago. I've been experimenting with my glasses, and if I get them in one position and hold my head at a certain angle, I can see the words no matter what size they are. Louise says she'll arrange for me to go over to St. Albert's when the eye doctor comes down next April. She says that once the doctor knows the problem, there's sure to be glasses that will work. But I don't know a lot of words, and I don't know how to write them down. I used to know, so I only need a bit of practice."

"Goodness gracious, Issy, you mean you haven't been able to see? Didn't the eye doctor check you for reading when you got your glasses?"

"No," I said, remembering how I managed to squirm out of the reading tests by having a little tantrum and screaming at the doctor that all of this stuff was just too *boring*.

"Let me think, Issy, let me think. I'll talk to your sister and Miss Simms, but I think this means we have to start back at the beginning. We can do it, Issy, I know we can. Are you willing to work harder than you've ever worked in your life? We have to collapse all your grades into a few weeks."

I nodded. But it turned out to be much more difficult than I ever imagined.

CHAPTER SEVEN

Bibby: a small tin kettle with large,
flat bottom tapering to the top

There was a sudden thaw in early March right after a terrible snowstorm that smashed power lines and plunged us into darkness for two days. I used the storm to catch up on my sleep and to rest my weary eyes. For three weeks Beryl had been on my back every night, and after she went home exhausted, Louise gave me extra homework to do. There were many, many times when I was so tired that I wanted to lash out at everyone, especially Beryl and Louise, but I held my temper, because I was old enough to know they were doing their best to help me.

When the lights came back on, the big news on TV was that our prime minister, Pierre Trudeau, had married young Margaret Sinclair, or Maggie as she soon came to be known. Louise and Mother were fascinated by every detail of the surprise wedding—her hooded dress, the small secret ceremony, the flowers she wore in her hair, the honeymoon.

The thaw meant that the ice moved out of the river in one big swoosh. We would get more ice—winter would go on until the end of May—but after a big thaw like that the river wouldn't be safe for skating again this winter. We had to move to the shallow ponds, which were still quite frozen. Beryl let me play hockey with the boys on Saturday and Sunday afternoons for an hour or so, and then it was back to the books. It was good fun, and I found myself grinning foolishly whenever I'd make a brilliant save.

At first Beryl brought along her little sister's books from school, and that's where we started. I knew what the letters looked like, but I hadn't written them down in years, so I practically had to learn how to hold a pen again. After a few weeks, holding the pen just so, with my glasses halfway down my nose and my head tilted at the angle of a bird eating a fat worm, I could print all the letters and was learning how to spell words from the grade two, three and four spelling books. Beryl was also reading to me from the grade nine history and geography textbooks. She said there was no way I would be able to catch up in time for the final exams unless we moved ahead on two fronts. I had always had a good memory, and once something was read to me I had it in my brain. Her goal was to get me to pass grade nine. Beryl said it didn't matter if I got just 50 percent in every subject, I simply had to pass. It seemed pretty hopeless to me, but I kept at it because Beryl wouldn't let me stop.

Wish dropped by occasionally, but I managed to keep secret from him what Beryl and I were doing. His mood had changed since the time we went to his house. He never invited us back again, he stopped playing hockey, and if Beryl wasn't around when he dropped in there'd be long patches of dead silence. No more

Cherry Blossoms, either. He seemed to be brooding about something, like he'd been just after the accident, but I could never find the right words to ask him what was going on in his head.

I spent a few minutes each day in the cemetery. Being with Lady was still the thing that gave me the most comfort. Sometimes I would sit there, near her grave, and just take in the rocky hills and the long, jutted bay. On a clear day I could see the church steeples in the zigzag of towns that hugged the shorelines. On cold, wet days Bush would huddle closer to me, reminding me that there was a perfectly warm house not too far away.

I began to while away the time in the graveyard by scraping the snow off tombstones around Lady's and practising my reading. I learned a lot about our place by reading a few words from the past. I found a man who'd survived three wives: *Separation is our lot, meeting again is our hope.* There was a girl who died when she was eighteen: *In short measure, life may perfect be.* I found Wish's mother and father in the same grave, with their names inside intertwining roses: *To live in the hearts of those we love is not to die.* They were only thirty-four and thirty-five when they died. I discovered three plaques to the memory of eighteen-year-old boys who died in the first war, and a small stone column inscribed with the names of eight men who died for Great Britain in the second war. None of the bodies had come home; they were all "buried on foreign soil." There was a memorial cross for one man who died in the Korean War: *Doing his duty.* There was a memorial for three men who disappeared when I was seven: *They are not dead, they are away.* I remembered the winter storm and the loss—a father and two grown sons who tried to cross the river at night, just a couple of hundred yards, but full of treachery. Everyone knew how hard it was to tell the difference between black water and black ice on a starless night.

One family grave made me thankful for the modern life we enjoyed.

Emma May
December 6, 1887–March 15, 1888

Edna Lillian
March 3, 1886–December 15, 1890

Hazel Irene and Rebecca Mabel
April 19, 1891–January 27, 1892

Samuel William
November 21, 1905–January 25, 1906

I did the math. The eldest had not lived to see her fifth birthday. The youngest child was dead at six weeks. That family grave was near the gate and it always made me sad as I walked home.

While I slaved away at my school work, Louise seemed bent on another journey, into the good doctor's mysterious heart. Dr. David was coming to the house at least once a week to check on Mother. I knew when he was expected by the flurry of activity in the kitchen. Louise was like a tornado; nothing was left unmoved or unwashed. The very stovetop was like a mirror and the stainless steel kettle was a dizzying pool of reflection. Matching vases of plastic red roses found their way to the chesterfield end tables, and Louise sewed new curtains for the living room and the kitchen.

A coffee percolator appeared on the counter. Specially blended coffees were stored in new wooden boxes and put in different cupboards so their flavours wouldn't contaminate each other. While the doctor was an Englishman and loved his tea, Louise learned that he much preferred coffee in the afternoons, and he usually managed to fit in a visit to Mother at supper-time—or tea time as they called it—when he came across the river to visit his growing list of patients. Somehow Louise always knew when he was in Riverbank making his rounds, and she poured his coffee when she heard the front gate click back on its hinges. Milk—not canned evaporated milk, but real milk—was ready at hand in one of Mother's fancy crystal milk jugs. He would take his coffee, and one poured for Mother, into the bedroom and stay long enough for Louise to do the final touches to the evening meal.

Supper now was different from anything we had experienced before. We all ate what Mother was supposed to eat, because the doctor said that to tempt a woman on a diet was a terrible thing. The potatoes were mashed with chicken broth, the fat was removed from all the meat, and the skin was taken off the chicken. Gravy was a light froth that somehow tasted good. We stopped baking entirely, and dessert was canned fruit, usually peaches or fruit cocktail. If Mother didn't come to the table for supper, as she sometimes did now, Louise let me put a bit of English clotted cream on my fruit on the understanding that not a word was said about it.

It was still too soon to notice if Mother was losing weight. The doctor said even a pound a week was a victory, so I could only guess that there was less of her each week as we won each small battle over french fries and double fudge chocolate layer cake with fudge icing. We knew it was going to be a long haul.

Mother was putting up with the diet because she had no choice. If she wanted anything else to eat, she would have to make it herself, and that wasn't going to happen.

My belts were getting loose. I had long been a big girl. I liked to think I wasn't fat, but my middle was thicker than most girls' my age at school.

Mother took out her frustration with her diet by sharpening her tongue. "Louise, let that poor doctor get on with his work, he doesn't want to talk to you." "Louise, I notice the kitchen floor could use a good scrub. Have you been using a mop again?" "Issy, the snow needs clearing off the back steps. I don't ask you to do much around here. You could keep your few chores in mind." "Louise, I have to have a scone. I don't care what the doctor says, one little scone is not going to hurt me. You and Issy have been sneaking them behind my back, haven't you?"

And so it went. Abuse heaped upon abuse, and no thought to what we were going through, running a house, taking care of an invalid, starving along with her, and keeping up with our school work. No matter—I was infected with Beryl's dream that I could read and even pass grade nine, and then I would be gone. So there.

ANOTHER WEEK of dreary hard work and another cold front. I shivered when I saw a fashion show on TV with models wearing the latest hot pants. I knew for certain that these tiny little outfits would make me look like a hippopotamus.

The cold froze everything up again. Out of the blue, after I hadn't seen him for a while and was starting to miss him, Wish dropped into our kitchen to say that Sergeant Fletcher had phoned over and wondered if anyone could take him ice fishing up in the ponds on the barrens. Wish had offered to take him and asked me if I wanted to go too. Just like that, did I want to spend a day on the barrens with him? I tried to say no, for a half second, but the word stuck in my throat. It happened to be the one Saturday that Beryl was going to Grand Falls and Louise was going to St. Albert's, so I'd be free as a seagull.

"Yes, I'd like that," I said, almost looking him full in his face as it flushed with unexpected pleasure. Surely he didn't think I *wouldn't* go to the barrens with him, the place where we had so many happy days as children?

He reached his hand across the table and touched mine, a lovely light touch that sent tingles shooting through my body. I could tell myself over and over that I didn't care about Wish, but my body still did silly things when he was close.

"I need a day out," I said, "to blow away the cobwebs."

I don't know what I said that was wrong, but he snatched away his hand, stood up quickly and reminded me to bring the teakettle on Saturday.

The sergeant was over our way lots of times during the winter. A fishing boat had mysteriously gone missing and he had to write a report for the insurance company. There was a bit more paper-work to do for the award nominations, and he was painfully meticulous about getting each detail in the right sequence. He came to Riverbank a couple of times to give the older grades a little lecture on drugs. "Know Your Enemy" was the theme. The girls thought he was the cutest cop they had ever seen, and taking a look at him while he told us the evils of marijuana and LSD, I could see why they were swooning over him. He was lean, all muscle, well over six feet tall, and there were laugh crinkles around his deep brown eyes. He had got used to us and our ways, and had no trouble drinking the instant coffee handed to him by our teacher.

On Saturday, we met at ten o'clock at the brook that runs down from the barrens, and for the first hour we followed the brook back up to the swimming hole used by the kids of Riverbank. Wish hardly paid me any attention, not even a smile. The sergeant too was lost in his own thoughts. Another hour, and we were crossing the open land on hard-packed snow. We barely talked. The walk itself was a challenge and we were carrying backpacks with our food and fishing gear. Besides, when you go with guys, it's not about the talking, it's about the fishing.

By one o'clock, after seeing a red fox cut across our path in the distance, we were at the edge of the frozen pond that had never let me down when it came to catching fish in winter.

Again, very little talk. Wish hardly looked at me but set off to find the fixings for a fire, and the sergeant got out his axe to chop three holes in the ice, which was a good foot thick. I was left to sort through the bags to see what we had for lunch; there's no avoiding women's work. Wish came back with dry kindling taken from the underbelly of old, dead trees, and he didn't insult me by suggesting he would make the fire. He went to prepare the lines so we could be fishing by the time lunch was ready.

We had sandwiches, apples, date squares and hermit cookies, the easiest things to eat out in the woods, so the only chore was to heat water for a mug-up. The bibby was bubbling by the time the lines were set. I threw in a handful of loose tea. The best tea in the world is made over an open fire in a battered kettle. The old-timers swore the kettle had to be covered in black soot, too.

The sergeant came over to the fire to warm his hands and took a Thermos out of his bag. "Coffee," he said, and when he opened it I got a whiff of the kind of coffee Louise made for the doctor.

We had to quit fishing much sooner than we expected, because the rainbow smelt were biting too fast. Poor things, they must have been hungry, and a good hunk of pork fat was more than they could resist. Now in truth, Wish and I might have kept on fishing, but when you're out fishing with an officer of the law you keep to the quotas. There was a time when we were kids that Wish and I had each caught over a hundred smelt in this pond in one afternoon. We caught each other's eyes, both remembering that afternoon. Neither of us bragged about this little episode to Sergeant Paul.

When we got back to town, Wish whispered that I should ask the sergeant to supper and fry up some of his fish for him. For a moment in time I thought Wish would come for supper too, but as soon as I asked the sergeant, Wish said his grandfather was expecting him and that he had to hurry along. I watched his back as he disappeared into the shadows and felt a sense of loss. The sergeant accepted the second-hand invitation so quickly, I had to wonder if that was what the whole day had been about.

"He's got something on his mind," Paul said as Wish went off into the darkness. "He'll come back to you."

I was so surprised by the sergeant's comment that I turned on my heel and dashed into the house. Surely he must see that we were only friends!

LOUISE WAS HOOKING a yellow rug for the kitchen when I ducked in just before the sergeant. She thought I was having a fit as I jerked my head back to flag that someone was coming in behind me.

"Oh," was all she said as she quickly tidied up the bits of wool all over the wing chair. "Coffee, ah, sir?" she asked as she walked toward the kitchen.

"Call me Paul, please, and no, I think I'll pass on the coffee. Your sister here said she would fry some of my fish for me. Is that okay?"

Louise knew I wouldn't have said any such thing, but she was fiddling with the fancy coffee percolator like she hadn't heard him say no. He raised his eyebrows when he saw it.

"Perhaps a cup of coffee would be nice after all. Now, Issy, hand me the fish you're going to cook, and I'll take them outside and gut them."

Mother could see the back step from her bedroom window and it wasn't long before she was calling down the hall to ask who that strange man was. Louise ignored her. It was the first time I'd ever seen her do that. Once the fish were frying, Mother's curiosity got the better of her. She'd wrapped herself in a loose housedress and then put a terry towel bathrobe over it and came out to the kitchen. The first thing I noticed was that the outfit she was wearing used to be tight across her behind, but now it fell in a straight line.

Her eyes almost popped out of her head when she saw a handsome man sitting at our kitchen table eating fish and potatoes and keeping Louise amused with silly stories about being a cop. I acted like I wasn't listening by staring into space and twirling the ends of my hair, but no way was I going to miss one sentence of a single story.

Mother pulled up a chair to sit down and Louise got her a small plate of the fish fry-up. Mother was so thrilled to be eating something close to normal that she forgot to be mean to Paul. I'd heard stories from Mildred's mom about how Mother had scared off a couple of good men who had been keen on Louise when she was young.

Mother sat with us while Paul talked about finding two thieves who broke into the Legion by following their footprints through the freshly fallen snow, and the time he had to fly back from Labrador in a small plane with a corpse, but the corpse wouldn't sit in the seat and kept jerking around. He had us all in stitches, laughing until our bellies hurt. We hadn't laughed together as a family in a long, long time.

The whole time he talked, he never once took his eyes off Louise. And surely I didn't see my sister bat her eyelashes at the sergeant—the idea was so silly I refused to believe it.

THAT WAS THE FIRST TIME I got a peek at the girl my mother used to be. She sat there eating her little bits of fish and drinking cup after cup of coffee sweetened with saccharine, and she didn't say an unkind word. Later, after Louise rooted through the cupboards and found a box of Purity Lemon Creams with caraway seeds, and let Mother have just one with the faintest smear of butter, Mother told one of her stories that turned out to be quite funny. It was about her coming to Newfoundland and bringing only four evening dresses with her, because Dad told her she wouldn't be needing many.

"I figured four would get me through the first season, you see." We laughed so hard that Louise and I had to pound each other on the back.

"Tell them about your dad letting you drive his big Bentley car when you were fourteen, or about that clock in London called Big Ben and the time it stopped working and you missed your train and your father sent the police to look for you," said Louise, demanding stories about Mother's life in England that I had never heard.

Paul left around eleven. He had a cold boat ride ahead of him across the river and then a cold vehicle to warm up, but he didn't seem to mind. The three of us shuffled off to bed. I think Mother put her hand on my shoulder as we went down the hall, but I couldn't be sure, the touch was so light.

After we crawled into bed and turned off the lamp, the coffee wouldn't let us sleep. That night, Louise told me about the mother she grew up with.

"I wonder if Mother was pretty when she was young?" I said into the dark.

"She was, I can remember when she looked quite lovely," said Louise. "I don't think anyone would have called her a beauty, but she had great bone structure and a good height. She had a pretty way of doing her hair. She'd pile it on top of her head and pin it there so that her natural curls fell down over her forehead. You wouldn't remember, but if you ever see a photo of Betty Grable, her hair was like that.

"Dad was around a lot in those days and we had a pretty normal life. We had lived in England until I was five years old, and he was away a lot then because of the war. When he first got the job at the electric plant, he was here all the time. Then when he went on the steamers, he came home for a week every month. Mother baked and cooked and cleaned house, I went to school."

"Then I came along and changed everything."

"No, not at all. She was sick long before she had you. She wanted to go back to England for a visit, and Dad was putting money aside so she could. He knew she needed to go. I was about eleven at the time. The big surprise was that Dad saved enough so I could go with her. It was my dream to go back to England, and I was so excited I didn't sleep for a week. About a month before we were to leave, we went to Grand Falls to get smallpox vaccinations. I hardly made it home before I got very, very ill. Dad had to turn around and take me back to the hospital. I was there for two weeks. Dad wanted Mother to go without me, but she wouldn't.

"Then something very odd happened. Dad met up with one of his old pals from before the war quite by accident, and he found out that Mother's parents were dead. Her father had been digging in his rose garden in London and hit a bomb that had dropped there during the war. He and Grandmother were killed outright, and several of the neighbours were injured. We wouldn't have known a thing about it if Dad hadn't met his old friend, who was doing a geographical survey of Newfoundland for the British government in 1948.

"Mother was stunned and very hurt. Things just went from bad to worse. I think that's when she realized she was here in Newfoundland forever, that she had no home to go to anymore except the one she made here. I kept saying she and I could go to England for a visit, but she lost all interest in going back. I started cooking the meals, cajoling her to get dressed, making her special desserts to entice her to eat. Up until then, her four evening dresses had hung in her closet, getting dusty and dated to be sure, but the following winter she asked me to pack them into a steamer trunk for her and put them in the shed.

"That was the beginning, only I didn't know it then. I thought it was just a bad spell. Dad came home less and less, she stayed in bed longer and longer, and ate more and more. I got through high school even though boarding over in St. Albert's was a real problem. I had to come home every weekend, no matter how stormy the weather, to tidy the house and cook Mother her meals for the next week. Mother would phone me every night while I was in boarding, crying and berating me for leaving her alone. When I won the scholarship to Memorial, she pulled herself together somehow and insisted she could manage on her own. Then I got a summer job in St. John's. I wasn't at all surprised when I got the call about her being in hospital.

"However, you can't imagine the shock I received when I got handed a *baby* when I walked in the door. I tried, you know, Issy. If you hadn't been so cross and contrary, it might have been okay."

I didn't say anything. What could I say? She was right. I heard Louise take a deep breath.

"Now I blame myself. All these years we thought you were so dumb, and it was your eyes. I am going to write to the government and complain about the young doctors they send around every two years to check eyes in the schools. They all missed your problem. You'd think someone might have noticed." Then she ended in a whisper. "Tonight, I realized my life here isn't so bad. Mother was a bit like her old self. You are overcoming your difficulties, and I laughed again. Maybe things are getting better."

I, too, had a think about my life there in the gloom of our bedroom. I couldn't help but feel that the amazing changes taking place in our lives all went back to the accident. We'd met the handsome RCMP officer who made Louise laugh, the doctor who got on Mother's case about her health and her diet—and who might well become her son-in-law—and Wish and Beryl had come into my life. It was a lot for one winter.

Soon we drifted off to sleep.

A WEEK LATER, I was doing my best to study for a history multiple-choice test when the doctor came by to see Mother. I should have known he was expected, because the coffee was perking and the little silver tray with the sugar bowl and milk jug was sitting on the kitchen counter.

Louise handed him his coffee and he brushed past me to visit with Mother. He was halfway down the hall before he turned and gave me a long, thoughtful look. After he took Mother's blood pressure and checked her weight on our new scale, he sat down for supper and took out his papers and wrote notes in files without seeming to notice we were at the table with him.

He was just a tiny bit boring, and as soon as I could, I went back to my studying. I noticed he was watching me again, as I was craning my neck to find the right angle to see the words on the page.

"What are you doing, for heaven's sake, child?" he said, startling me so much I knocked my glasses off my face.

Louise spoke up for me. "Issy has had some difficulties seeing. She found out a few weeks ago that if she holds her head just so, she can see the words on the page. The eye doctor will be down this way in a couple of weeks for her to get new glasses."

"Come here," he commanded, very much in his doctor voice. He reached into his black bag and took out a light and told me to look all over the place while he shone the thing into my eyes. He had me try to read the Irving calendar at the other side of the kitchen and a piece of paper he put in front of me. Then he took my glasses off my face, searched for another instrument in his bag and measured the glass. "These glasses are absolutely useless to you for reading. How long have you been wearing them?"

"Almost two years for those—the doctor comes down to St. Albert's every two years. But she's been wearing specs since she was five years old," Louise answered. She was hovering behind his back, and he turned to her.

"Her pupil isn't aligned properly. It happens sometimes. Most children get it fixed by the time they're two, and that's the end of it. I can't believe the operation wasn't done years ago. It's very minor surgery but won't fix the droop in her eyelid—we like to wait until they're older to fix that. How old are you, child?"

I wanted to tell him I had a name, but I was shaking all over. Was he saying my eye could be fixed?

"She's almost sixteen, Doctor," said Louise.

"I did hundreds of these while I was in surgery in London. It's about the same level of difficulty as tying a shoelace. I suggest you get her to Grand Falls as soon as you can and get her eye checked by a proper specialist. She's old enough to have the realignment and the plastic surgery to fix the droop in her eyelid at the same time. Poor child—she can't have seen very well close up since she was born. It'll be a whole new world for her." And with that, he patted me on the knee, wrote out instructions on a prescription pad and gave them to Louise.

"I expect they'll fit her with contact lenses once she's all fixed up. New research shows that contacts improve the vision better than glasses in cases like this. She's done an amazing job of adapting if you haven't noticed that she can't see up close."

A look of guilt passed over Louise's face when I looked at her with a question in my eyes.

"Will it hurt her, Doctor?" she asked.

"Like your eye is burning a hole in your face," he said to me with just a trace of humour, "but only for a day or two, and after a couple of weeks of patching you're going to be so pleased at what you're seeing, you won't notice anymore."

But nothing is as easy as it sounds.

LOUISE PHONED the hospital to make an appointment. They said the next one available for an evaluation was in September, and if that went well, surgery could happen as early as December—more

than a half year away. I stomped around the kitchen and back and
forth to the living room and my bedroom for the entire evening
after Louise told me the news. I made sure everyone knew I was
upset.

"I thought it was all going to happen next week. I thought the
doctor said I was an urgent case. I thought he said I had to have it
done as soon as possible," I hissed at Louise every chance I got.

She let me blow off steam before saying, "Settle down, Issy.
September is 'as soon as possible.' You're not on death's door, for
goodness' sake. You've managed for fifteen years, you can wait a bit
longer. What difference does it make?"

Well, that little pep talk drove me further around the bend. By
this time Mother was thumping her walking stick on the floor the
way she did whenever she heard us cat fighting.

"Now look what you've done. I had Mother settled down for the
night," Louise said as she jumped up to see what Mother wanted.

I grabbed her arm. "Can't you ask Dr. David to do something?"
I pleaded.

"No way, Issy. You don't take advantage of friendships like that.
He's doing so much for Mother already, I don't want to ask for
more."

I flung myself on my bed and burst into tears. "What difference
does it make?" Louise had asked. Well, to me it was the whole
world, and why couldn't she see that? What was the sense of me
working so hard when nobody cared about me? It was always
Mother this and Mother that. Beryl and Louise were pushing me
too hard with the homework, it was still hard seeing the words,
and I was getting headaches from the strain. Why was I bothering

anyway? I asked myself. Who was I trying to impress? Dad didn't care one way or the other, Mother didn't for sure, and Louise just wanted me to succeed so I could take care of Mother and she could marry the doctor without feeling guilty about it.

I pushed my head into my pillow and curled up against the wall. It didn't take long before Bush jumped up on the bed, curved his body into mine and pushed his nose into my neck. Then I felt his paw digging into my back. "Don't turn your back on me" was what he was saying, and I had to turn then and laugh. As I did so, I got a whiff of him. He smelt like an outhouse! He needed a bath, and he needed it right there and then.

"Come on, you awful dog," I said as I tried to lift him off the bed. "We need to give you a nice quiet bath. We can't wake Mother, you know, because she may have a heart attack if we do." I bundled up my bedspread for the wash. No way was that going to get close to my body tonight.

Bush did not like baths, and he recognized the word. I had to drag him by his collar to the kitchen, where I filled up our old galvanized wash tub with warm water. Now, Bush wasn't much of a barker, so I knew I was pretty safe trying to bathe him at ten o'clock at night, and besides, by this time Louise was reading, tucked away in Dad's room, where she'd set up a comfortable chair and a bright lamp. She never heard a thing once she was reading.

"Bush, you filthy dog, come here right now," I said as he looked at me, feet firmly planted on the floor, his big head tilted and his sad brown eyes begging me to understand that dogs do not have baths.

I grabbed him by the collar and pulled him toward the water. He kept his legs stiff and his head down. I was going to have to lift him into the bath if this was going to work. Bush had to be eighty pounds and it was going to be a challenge. But he smelt so foul, like he'd rubbed himself in moose dung, that if he didn't have a bath, he'd have to go outside, and it was well below zero out there.

I had got Bush about a foot away from the tub when the back-porch door opened quietly.

"I was out walking and saw the kitchen light on. What are you doing? Hi there, Bush. Something smells real bad." It was Wish.

I'd hardly talked to Wish since his granddad went all haywire after he found out I was a Heffernan. We'd had the Saturday with the sergeant, and there was once our paths would have crossed up on the barrens if I hadn't hidden quickly and taken another route. He looked so unhappy at the time that I couldn't deal with it.

I was surprised that Beryl had kept up with my lessons. I thought the whole point was so she could see Wish. But she hadn't said a word about it.

"I think he rolled in some kind of dung. He's got to have a bath and he's refusing to get into the water," I said.

"You're doing it all wrong, that's why. You've got to trick him. He's a retriever. Throw a ball into the water, for heaven's sake," said Mr. Know-It-All.

The idea did kind of make sense. I found his rubber ball and nonchalantly tossed it into the water. Well, Bush was absolutely comical. You could see him thinking, "The ball is in the water, I want the ball, so now what do I do?" I picked up the ball and tossed it in again. "Ah," thinks Bush, "this is a game, I like this game," and *splash,* he was in the tub.

"Here, you soap him down while I play with him," said Wish. Bush didn't stay still for one second, half the time jumping for the ball and the other half diving for it in the water. The whole front of me was wet by the time I was towelling Bush off. Wish was pretty soaked too.

"You can't go home like that, sit down and I'll make you a cup of tea. I've got some cookies hidden away, too," I said.

Louise came out of Dad's room then and put her fingers to her lips, reminding me not to wake Mother. "Hello, Wish. I'm going to bed, Issy, I'm beat." She slipped down the hall and into our room.

I'd actually been hoping she could stay. Wish and I had not been alone together for a long time, and I wasn't looking forward to it, especially since he seemed so gloomy.

But Wish wanted to talk. That's when I found out that I was not the only one in confusion about staying put or leaving home.

WE ENDED UP SITTING side by side on the couch. I headed for the leather wing chair, but Bush eased his bones and his wet fur into it before I could get there. So I had to sit on the couch beside Wish, and then Bush took the measure of the situation and right away jumped off the wing chair and got in between me and Wish to close the gap. He was in dog heaven as Wish and I both petted his broad back and tickled him around the ears. Maybe it was the darkness—there was only a gleam of light from the kitchen—or maybe the closeness and warmth of Bush, but Wish opened up his heart that night. I listened.

"I told Aunt and Uncle that I was coming back here for the best part of a year. They didn't like it one bit. We had a couple of sessions in their den with both of them talking at me, saying that after all they had done for me they couldn't believe I wanted to throw it all away and go back to a hick town in Newfoundland.

"I told them I appreciated everything, that I knew private schools cost a great deal of money, that I realized not everyone gets offered a full scholarship to university.

"Uncle hinted at a partnership waiting at his law firm and how I was their only heir.

"I told them lots of people in Riverbank had honest jobs in the inshore fishery, at the power plant and in the woods, but that got them so upset I had to take another tack.

"I told them how all I ever wanted was to go back to Newfoundland in the summers. I was twelve when Mom and Dad died, you remember, Issy? I wasn't a baby who would forget them in a haze of pampering. Aunt and Uncle kept sending me off to wilderness camps instead. I hated every second of it, lakes are not the same thing as the ocean, and several times I considered running away. I think Aunt was afraid that if she sent me back here, she'd lose me. And she might have been right. I wanted to be with Granddad and ask him about Dad growing up. I needed Granddad to show me about the fishing and boats and how to build a house. That's what the boys learn here. Instead I have soft hands and no idea how you measure out a basement or choose a piece of land or find the best place for a well.

"My uncle was quick to remind me that a lawyer can work to help people in many ways, and I knew he was right, and I almost gave up. But Issy, then I remembered the river and, well, all my old friends." (Did he really have to look at me so softly from under his lashes?)

"Chris Joe is getting married in the summer and he's got his house half built. He's only two years older than me and was one of my best friends when I was a youngster.

"I made them a promise. I told Aunt and Uncle that if they let me come with good hearts, I'd go to university next September.

"Now I'm not sure I can keep that promise. Six months has gone by like a moment in time. The manager of the power plant has offered me a job, starting off as a labourer but with the likelihood I could apprentice as an electrician. I'd be earning my own money and wouldn't be dependent on Aunt and Uncle. I'm almost nineteen. Granddad is very sick. I should have been home every one of those summers."

I was having trouble believing that Wish was whipping himself for decisions that were taken out of his hands. I tried to say just that. "Wish, you were too young," I said.

"Don't even think that," he hissed with such force that Bush's ears went straight up. "I wanted to be given everything, just like any other kid. I wanted the bikes and the skis and the trips to Florida. I was trapped before I knew it. Aunt and Uncle adopted me and I was their 'darling boy.' I'm not a Sweetapple anymore in Toronto, you know, and no one calls me Wish up there. I'm Alfred Higgins-Jones. They said Alfred would be better because Aloysius is so old-fashioned. I guess it is a bit old—it's the name of the first Sweetapple to settle in Newfoundland two hundred years ago." I could hear the pride in his voice.

His teacup was empty and I made a fuss about pouring him another cup from the pot I'd brought to the coffee table. I even put in his milk and a teaspoon of sugar. I was buying time; I needed every second I could get to try to understand why someone as smart as Wish would want to stay here in Riverbank, an isolated and lonely place where the world passed you by. Thoughts of Lady flashed through my brain—she'd seen the world and came home to live a much smaller life—and my dad, who always came back, time after time, despite everything. Why, I wondered, did they come back when there was so big a world out there? What was pulling at Wish and making it so difficult for him to go?

Finally I broke the silence with the only thing I could think of saying. "Why would you want to stay here, Wish? Just about everyone wants to go to the mainland the moment they can."

"You're such a kid, Issy. Everything is rush, rush, rush in Toronto. Here it's so peaceful and calm, you can take the time to make things, like these cookies. No one bakes in Toronto, no one has the time anymore.

"But I made a promise, and a promise is a promise. I know they just want me to be happy."

And with that the room went quiet again. There was nothing I could say. He had wanted to lay it all out and have another go at sorting through it.

Then he weighed up his life again. "I like to travel, to see things, to read new books, see plays, go see the Leafs play at Maple Leaf Gardens. I miss the hockey games I played every Saturday morning with my school friends. I just don't know if I can last down here. I love lots of things about Riverbank, but I need the big city too. Maybe I'm spoiled for this life."

I knew he didn't want me to tell him what to do. "What's wrong with your granddad?" I asked to change the subject.

"He's going funny in the head, and he gets very tired. He forgets things. Sometimes he asks me who I am. Sometimes he talks about his past like it happened that morning. Last week he got me up in the middle of the night to tell me to go lock all the doors because drug addicts were trying to get in. I tried to calm him by telling him there were no drug addicts in Riverbank, but in the end I had to go and make like I was locking every door and window. He forgot about it the next day."

"Did he ever say anything more about the Heffernans and the Sweetapples?"

"No, and I don't dare ask him. I don't want to set him off again."

"When do you have to decide about the job at the power plant?"

"There's no hurry on that. Mr. Brake said I could take a bit of time to think it over," he answered, stifling a yawn.

By this time Bush was fast asleep and the house was ghostly silent. Wish—I could only think of him as Wish—stretched.

"I need to get going. Look, old buddy, thanks for listening to me. I've never met anyone who is a better listener than you." He grabbed my hand and brought it to his lips. "It's a gift, you know, being able to listen. You have a pure heart, Issy," he said, looking into my eyes. "Now tell me something. When I came in, you had been crying—your eyes were puffy and your nose was red. Your nose always gets red when you've been crying. Tell me who made you cry and I'll go beat them up right now," he said with a chuckle in his throat.

I couldn't say a word. He was still holding my hand, and as long as Wish held my hand I couldn't breathe, and you have to breathe to speak.

Then a wild animal must have got close to the yard, because Bush woke up and sprang to the porch door and broke the spell.

"I'm fine, Wish, just fine," I said in a raspy whisper as we got up and I reached for his coat and scarf on the back of the couch to hand them to him. I couldn't tell him about the operation, because then I would have to tell him about not being able to read.

"Wow," I said, "this scarf feels really nice. What is it made of, some highfalutin Toronto material?"

He laughed as he took it. "No, silly, just cashmere."

I didn't know what cashmere was at the time, and when I did, I thought back to that night when I used a cashmere scarf to dry Bush off after his bath.

I WENT FOR A LONG WALK along the river path the next day after school. There was just enough light reflected from the river for me to see where I was going. It was a dreary, wet day and the heavy darkness spread early. I didn't want to tell Beryl I was through with the lessons, that I didn't want to do them until I could see properly. I couldn't tell her to her face because I knew she would find a way to convince me to stay put. I thought she would take the hint if I just didn't show up.

I ended up in the cemetery and sat with Lady for a bit, until the damp started to come up through the stone. It was so comforting to be near her. Then I dropped in on Mrs. John and got her a bowl of soup and continued down to the far end of the cove to see

Mildred and her mother. I walked down the hill to home as slowly as I possibly could.

"Beryl was here for the longest time," Louise said as I walked in. "She left just a few minutes ago. Your supper is in the oven keeping warm, just a bit of corned beef and carrots and turnips. I was waiting for you to come home to go for potatoes, and in the end I did supper without them." She darn well knew I was still upset.

"Look, Issy, there are things in life that cannot be changed. You need to learn to buck up and get on with it. You can still learn to read without the operation. You were getting along fine until the doctor said your eye could be fixed." Louise put the hot plate in front of me.

I let my hair drift over my face. I didn't want another round of what I could be doing and what I should be doing. I fed Bush my supper when Louise went to see to Mother, and then I went to bed. I needed a good night's sleep.

On Wednesday, Beryl caught up with me before class started. "Issy, I waited for you last night. I thought we had a date," she said, blue eyes widened in a question.

"I made up my mind on the weekend that I can't do it. I'm getting headaches. It's too much eye strain," I said. I had rehearsed this. I didn't want to hurt Beryl. Her heart was in the right place.

"Oh, Issy, I'm so sad to hear that. Why don't you take a few days' rest and we'll see how it goes next week? You were doing so well," she said in such a distressed voice that I thought she was going to hug me. No one ever hugged me—I didn't like people to get that close.

"Sure," I said, "next week." What a nuisance people are, I thought. You let them get close to you and then they don't know when to go away, when to back off, when to go fly a kite.

That was the day Miss Simms announced a surprise history quiz. I strained to listen to the instructions while trying to look indifferent by staring out the window at fluffy white clouds. I ignored the test at first and then, when everyone else had their heads down, I tilted my head, pushed my glasses down my nose and started reading the questions. I could pick out a few of the ones about dates, and I knew the answers. Who didn't know when Captain James Cook charted the waters around Newfoundland? I never had trouble remembering something if I heard it once, and Beryl had read the chapters on the quiz to me last week.

Just for fun, I picked up my pen and began to fill in some of the blanks, making small, careful, even strokes like I had been practising. I was only three-quarters of the way through when the bell rang for dinner. I put the test paper in the pile as I'd always done.

I remember the day of the history quiz for another reason too. It was the day Miss Simms asked for volunteers to organize the grade nine graduation ceremony. We waited for Beryl to put up her hand, and when that was done she turned directly to me and said, "I want my friend Issy to be the treasurer. She's got a great head for math."

I turned scarlet, of course. I had never been singled out or praised in public. The odd thing was that no one noticed, no one objected. Everyone went back to work, and when class was over, they gathered around Beryl to find out what jobs they'd be doing.

She managed to find something especially important for everyone who volunteered.

Miss Simms handed back the test results on Friday. I got 60 percent and a gold star.

CHAPTER EIGHT

Dory: a small, flat-bottomed boat with
flaring sides and sharp bow and stern

As the weather turned warmer in April, Louise turned up the heat on her pursuit of Dr. David. He mentioned on one of his visits that his all-time favourite thing in the whole world was a raisin scone hot out of the oven. Now, both Louise and I knew how to make English scones. Mother had taken the time from her sickbed to teach us that the dough was kneaded seven times and that it was best to cut it into triangles rather than make the scones round, like everyone else did. You got more crispy edges with the triangles. She said if you made them small enough, they could be used for afternoon tea or as special jam cakes when people came to call.

We stopped making the scones when Mother went on her diet. They were deadly, full of lovely butter. Then the doctor said he liked scones, and almost magically we had scones coming out of our ears. The freezer was full of them, more than we could ever eat. The doctor always ate two, still flaky-fresh, right out of the oven. I might have two, and Louise, who ate like a bird, nibbled on half of one. That left more than half of every batch for freezing. The trick was to get them into the freezer as fast as we could, so the smell didn't linger and upset Mother, who was forbidden to have any at all.

Whenever the coffee went on, a fresh batch of scones would go in the oven. Louise loosened her hair a bit, too, and put on a touch of lipstick. The doctor came often and stayed longer and longer each visit.

I couldn't tell if they were smitten with each other or if they each merely took a good look and decided that the other would do. There were no signs of romance; she didn't start wearing the latest fashions—platform shoes or a granny gown—and he didn't bring flowers or chocolates. They hardly looked at each other while they ate supper together, and he often continued with his paperwork while he ate. She usually had a book going and would read it at the table, propped up against the teapot.

I began to secretly cheer on the relationship. It was probably true that we shouldn't take advantage of a friend, but a brother-in-law might find out that my surgery was put on hold and he just might pull some strings for his sister-in-law. He looked comfortable enough in our home, and I even got to convincing myself that he would move in with us and I could go off and find my own life without having to steal away. Sure, they didn't even have to move in. Lady's house was just across the lane, sitting vacant, waiting, close enough to Mother.

Then I heard that the doctor was getting married. Smack out of the blue. At first I was annoyed, because I thought Louise might have told me something like that first before I had to hear it from Beryl. I ran all the way home with the shocking news.

My sister was sitting at the kitchen table, sipping coffee, staring at the wall somewhere between the Irving calendar and the tea towel hung up to dry.

"I know what you've heard," said Louise. "I know as little about it as you do. Shirley is a good woman and I'm sure they'll be very happy together."

Again I got a glimpse of my sister's courage. She even smiled, and joked about how we'd learned to make real coffee and got ourselves a freezer full of scones. But I knew she must be hurting, because even if her heart wasn't scorched, her pride was shredded.

The doctor came to visit Mother that day, but he didn't stay for supper. It was understood that his fiancée could get him his supper from now on.

He was marrying the latest Peterson "girl." Her name was Shirley Cameron. We used to call her Shirl, but now that she was to be the doctor's wife the name on everyone's lips was Shirley, full and proper. It turned out that while he loved English scones, he adored English fruitcake, and Shirley made the best fruitcake on the south coast of Newfoundland. She was a few months short of twenty-nine years old, which made her about five years younger than our Louise, and she had a full figure compared with Louise, who was as skinny as a scarecrow. Beryl told me that Shirley fawned over the doctor every time he visited, taking his coat and cleaning it for him, sometimes forcing him to take off his shoes so she could polish them, and feeding him plate after plate of fruit-cake. Hats off to Shirley, she knew how to get her man.

"I don't think I would have ever got used to him not looking me in the eye, anyway," said Louise a couple of days later.

As soon as the wedding plans were announced, we got more startling news. Mr. and Mrs. Peterson decided they weren't up to training another girl, they said "The era of servants is gone," so they were going to reduce the size of their shop and stay open for only two hours each evening. As of June, they were planning to sell only cigarettes, beer, bread and milk and candy. Beryl told me they wanted to spend more time developing their hunting and guiding business, which was worth a lot more money than a convenience store.

Once Louise heard that Peterson's was closing down, she pulled herself together and announced her own shocking news: she was going to buy a car. "Times change and we can change with them," she said as she briskly went through drawers to find her driver's licence, which she had faithfully renewed.

To buy a car was a big deal for us. Louise phoned Dad and told him what she was thinking of doing, and he said he'd better come home to help her pick one out.

As you will see, because the doctor married Shirley Cameron, I ended up getting an earlier appointment to have my eye fixed. It all worked out for me in the end—rather better than I expected, really.

DAD HAD NEVER LOOKED so good to me. I saw his tall limbs unfolding from the little dory that Mr. Jeddore used to ferry people back and forth, and I wanted to run down to the wharf like I used to when I was a child. Instead, I forced myself to wait for him to come up the lane, but I didn't move from the window.

He was a very good-looking man. He was different this trip because his hair was longer. It curled down over his ears and made him look more like a pirate than a responsible engineer. He stood straight, his body was lean. He walked with a fluid ease, like a satisfied cat. I got my hazel eyes flecked with gold from Dad. I got my dark, wavy hair from him too. He swung his duffle bag and suitcase like they were matchboxes and waved to everyone, and I knew he would be smiling that open smile that reached out to everyone within hailing distance. Every family in Riverbank where the men went away to work treasured the days they were home.

He said a quick hello to me in the kitchen, "I've got you a little something in my side pocket there," and loped down the hall to Mother. He always went to Mother first. They were good together for a couple of days. Then she'd get heart pains and he'd get the urge to move on.

I searched the pocket he'd pointed to in his suitcase and found two boxes, the same size. I shook both and they seemed to be the same. Then I noticed the tags and found the right position to read them. One was for me and the other for Louise. I opened mine and found a lovely silver charm bracelet with two charms already attached. One was a graduation cap and the other said *Sweet Sixteen*. It was the most touching gift my father had ever given me.

He came back down the hall with a look of deep concern on his face. "Has your mother not been well? Why didn't Louise tell me?"

I didn't know what he was talking about. "She's been fine, Dad. Same old same old. Thanks for the bracelet."

"It's nothing, baby doll." Baby doll! I was a child the last time he called me that. "I figured since your mother liked hers so much, it must be a good thing to buy girls these days. They're even selling charms on the boat now. I got yours in Sydney. They're real silver. It's for your birthday. But Mother looks sick—she's lost a lot of weight. Has the doctor checked her out good?"

"Oh, that. She's on a diet. The doctor said she had to lose weight—it was putting too much strain on her heart. She's been getting up more and more since she's been slimming down. Louise took in some of her dresses yesterday."

I asked him to help me with the clasp on the bracelet and then he swung me around. "Let me take a look at you, child. You've slimmed down too. All your baby fat has disappeared. You look like one of those fashion models on TV. Have you done something with your hair?"

I blushed. Fashion model—me! Only a dad would say such a thing. Beryl was helping me with my hair. She'd cut a bit off so it would take to curlers better, and it just so happened I had curled my hair the night before. Instead of unruly waves, it spread out over my shoulders in a glossy mass. I was amazed with how well it curled and shone.

I'd sneaked onto the scales in Mother's bathroom one evening and discovered I had lost five pounds. Mother must have lost twenty, but she still had another thirty to go. She was much better about it now. As the pounds dropped off, she spent more time looking at the dresses and pantsuits in the catalogues. Her face was thinner and I could see how she might once have been a lovely girl.

Louise loved her charm bracelet too. Dad, because he only knew how to be fair, had got her two charms as well. One was an apple that said *Teacher* and the other a little car. I couldn't wait to go to school on Monday with my new bracelet, though I did have a pang or two that I should keep it for my birthday, still more than two months away.

Dad had come home on Friday, and on Saturday, after much fussing, he and Louise took the bus to Grand Falls to buy a car. I was anxious all day. I kept telling myself that it was only a car, but the truth was, if I was real nice to Louise, she might let me get my licence when I turned sixteen. Summer was a perfect time to learn to drive. Then I would catch myself and remember that I had no intention of being here this summer.

They phoned home around six, Louise gushing over her almost-new Pontiac Tempest. She said they would have to stay overnight, that it took all day to get the paperwork done for the car and that Dad didn't want them driving two hours over a dirt road in early April when you never knew where there might be black ice or if a moose might wander out onto the road.

I had to take care of Mother overnight—the first time ever. It turned out not to be as bad as I feared. Dad had brought her a couple of charms too and she was in a good mood. She ate her chicken noodle soup like a lamb, watched TV for a little bit and asked me to get her ready for bed around eight o'clock. "I'm too excited to do anything but sleep. Imagine us having a car," she said.

Excited. I turned the word around on my tongue. It was not a word I had ever heard spoken by my mother.

The next morning, Mother shooed me out of the house and told me to go do whatever I did on Sundays. I went down to the wharf to see if I could catch sight of Dad and Louise and the car. Louise told me it was a gold colour. I was looking across the river so intently, I didn't notice Wish until he said hello almost in my ear. My body flinched at the surprise.

"Why are you so tense? Did you think I was an axe murderer or something?" he asked.

I shaded my eyes against the flat sunlight to look up at him. He still seemed so gloomy. I told him about the car and Dad being home.

"I always liked your father. He was kind to all the kids whenever he came home. You have his amazing eyes, you know, and the same grace when you move."

Now that was news to me. But awfully nice to hear.

"Hey, I'll drop over tonight, if that's okay. I'd like to see your father. Better still, why don't I borrow old Jeddore's boat and row us over to meet them? We can wait over there just as well as here."

Why didn't I think of that?

As I got up from the wharf, my new bracelet fell down over my wrist and perhaps I did shake it a tiny bit to hear it jangle. It caught Wish's eye right away.

"Hey, that's new, isn't it? Who's been giving my little friend charms?" he said as he reached out to look at them more closely.

"Now you're being silly. It's from Dad, of course. Who else!"

"'Sweet Sixteen.' I thought your birthday was in June. Isn't it June 21, Midsummer's Day?"

I couldn't believe he would remember that. And then I remembered something else: of course he would remember; we had the same birthday.

"Dad doesn't come home very often, so he got it for me early. I probably should put it away until June," I said with perhaps a touch of bitterness in my voice about my father's indefinite absences.

"Be thankful your dad comes home at all, little Issy," he said as he stared across the water. "The bracelet is pretty and pretty girls should wear pretty things and … isn't that a gold car pulling in on the landing? We'd better row like the dickens."

My heart was in a fuddle after that queer little speech from Wish, but we each took an oar and were across the river in record-breaking time.

Louise getting a car caused quite a stir in Riverbank. The fact that it was gold and snazzy, with power windows and an eight-track player, drove the mothers near crazy. Louise was supposed to be their mousy principal, the one who would be around forever. They had sighed with relief when the doctor chose Shirley Cameron, but now they had this to contend with—an unmarried woman with her own wheels. Heavens! Louise claimed she was forced into it because we had to buy groceries and we couldn't be beholden to the kindness of neighbours for every little thing we needed. It was awkward for her, she told me one night, being the principal; she couldn't put herself in a position where she needed favours.

But underneath all this very sound reasoning, I detected a Louise who loved that Pontiac. The keys glistened like silver stars on the kitchen counter. She had put in an order for a tape of Tom Jones's newest hit, "She's a Lady," and for one by the Rolling Stones, and she didn't mind washing dishes all day long because, while she was at the sink, she could look across the river and see the gleam of gold in the distance. When she got behind the wheel, she drove as if she had a tiger in her tank, like the old commercial on TV.

And Louise wasn't the only one who had loosened up a bit; Dad seemed a lot more relaxed on this trip. I couldn't figure out what was different at first. I thought it must be the car, because while Louise and I were in school, he was driving around the bay running family errands and doing the odd jobs that had piled up for what seemed like years. He got new linoleum for the kitchen floor and had it put down before we got home from school. He found hinges for the back door and threw away the ones that were almost rusted through. He replaced a pane of glass in our bedroom that was cracked and had rattled all winter. He cleared the dirty snow from the paths down to the gravel and knocked the last icicles of the winter off the eaves. One evening we came home and he was making a big pot of stew with a boiled raisin pudding on top.

"Don't look so shocked, my ladies. I live by myself most of the year—I know how to cook the basics," he said as we came in and smelt the food. "I found bags and bags of scones in the freezer and they go perfect with stew, so I decided to make up a batch."

All of this was wonderful, but something was niggling at me. By Wednesday I had it figured out: Dad was talking to us.

Mother was the only one who talked in our family. I mean that literally. Louise said next to nothing except when she wanted to taunt me or during our occasional late night sessions; I barely ever had two words to string together; and when Dad had come home in the past, his too was a silent world.

As I've mentioned, Dad's hearing wasn't too good. His ship had been torpedoed once in the war, and another time when his ship was hit by shellfire, he fell two decks and landed on his head. He thought that was when he lost his hearing. It wasn't totally gone, though. If you raised your voice well above normal and spoke into his good ear, which wasn't very good at all, he could make out what you were saying. Somehow he heard Mother best of all, but she too had to raise her voice to make him understand.

It was hard. As a child I learned to keep my sentences short, not to say anything unless it was vitally important, and to be guiltily happy when he went away and we didn't have to strain anymore to talk to him. I never told him any of my childhood troubles; it would have been too difficult to get it all said and to make him understand.

It was the stew that woke me up. There we were, having a normal family conversation around the supper table. And then I remembered that when Wish was over on Sunday night, they had talked about Toronto and the value of a good education. My father didn't go on about it in Riverbank, but he was a qualified marine engineer. Very few people his age had their papers. He studied to be an engineer for four years in Halifax after the war. He and Wish had talked like everything was, well, normal.

I looked at him closely and finally saw what I was looking for. Beneath the grey curls, there was something hooked over the back of his ear. I knew what to look for because blind old Mrs. John was also hard of hearing.

I couldn't help myself. "Dad, you're wearing a hearing aid!"

He was serving up seconds from the stew pot and looked at me a little abashed. "Can you see it, baby doll? I was hoping it was hidden under my hippie hair."

I told him that a person had to look real hard to see it, and that put the sparkle back in his eyes.

Over supper, he told Louise and me how difficult it was not being able to hear what people were saying to him. He said it hadn't been so bad at work in the past, because he was often down below deck and it was better not to hear the big engines. But as he was getting more senior, he was being invited to sit at the captain's table when special events were held at CN Marine, and it was becoming embarrassing when he couldn't follow the conversation.

"One night a doctor was on board the boat, turned out he was doing some special operation in Port aux Basques, and we got to talking that trip and then on his way back. He said it was possible that my hearing loss wasn't permanent. I went to see him in Sydney, he got me hooked up with a specialist, and he was able to do a little operation that restored about fifty percent of my hearing in one ear. Then he rigged me up with this hearing aid for my good ear. Almost like new. I keep telling Mother that she doesn't have to shout at me and she says that after more than thirty-five years it's hard not to."

I decided on a little test. In the past, rather than ask, I would get up from where I was sitting and walk around the table for anything I needed that was near Dad. "Could you pass the scones, Dad?" I asked.

"Of course, sweetie. Is that boyfriend of yours coming over tonight? I need a hand with the water pump."

I blushed about the "boyfriend" part, and while it wasn't true and I knew he was teasing me, it was marvellous to be teased by my dad.

"I'll help you with the pump, Dad," I said as he winked at me and handed across the plate of scones.

THE TRICK to fixing the pump was that you had to be prepared to lie on your stomach in a narrow crawl space in the cold mud under the house. Our house was big—down the hall to Mother's room was a hike—but we didn't have a basement because, except for a small root cellar dug out under the back porch, the house was built on bedrock. In the early days, when everyone on the island depended on the fishery, people built close to the water, and that's where we'd stayed. Just about the whole coastline of Newfoundland was rock and cliffs, so if you wanted to be near the water, you built on top of the rock.

We often waited for a nice dry spell to get at the pump so it wouldn't be as messy. But Dad was only home for two weeks, and he was bent on fixing it before he went back. It was important because, without it, we didn't have flush toilets or a shower. The pump had gone down a couple of times before, and the signs were the same now: you had to wait for the water to flow after turning on the taps, and occasionally there was no water at all for about ten seconds.

It was especially important to keep the pump in good working order because Mother depended on a hot bath every day; it was one of her little quirks. Most people got by on a bath once a week, but Mother said she had to give up many things when she came to

Newfoundland, and she absolutely refused to give up her daily soak in the tub. When Dad was building the house and decided to double its size, he had planned to change the second bathroom into a storage room, but that same week Mother was reading *Chatelaine* magazine and there was a homes feature about a bathroom off the master bedroom. *Chatelaine* called it an "ensuite." Dad did the math and said it wouldn't cost that much more, so why not have what the hotshots on the mainland had.

It turned out to be one of the wisest things he ever did. Over the years the only room Mother took any interest in looking warm and comfortable was her bathroom. It was a deep red (which I painted, four coats no less). It boasted a gold mirror and tall gold-coloured faucets ordered from Toronto. The old-fashioned bathtub had brass claws for feet, and there were a dozen big, fluffy towels with satin edges ordered from some swish store in London. Dad ran a wire from the antenna to her bedroom so she could have her own TV, and a little "loveseat" was ordered from St. John's. Quite the life. Everything was at Mother's fingertips.

Anyway, getting back to the pump. When Dad was home, he liked to keep Mother happy, and she'd been complaining about the water. So under the house I went, with Dad giving me instructions as I fiddled with the pump. A valve needed a new washer and a couple of stripped screws had to be replaced. I'd fixed the very same things a couple of times on my own, but it felt like we were a proper family with Dad handing me the screwdriver and the plumber's grease so I could loosen the screws.

I'm pretty sure I already said that Dad usually lasted about four days at home. But this time, with the car and Mother sitting up a bit more in her room, and perhaps because he could hear what was going on, it looked like he was going to make it for the whole two weeks. I hummed a bit as I fiddled with the screws and the valve. It was hard for me to see them, but I squinted until I got them lined up. That's when I realized I must have been doing that all my life, for all the things I needed to do. I finally gave the pump a whack with my screwdriver, the signal that I was finished. Dad pulled out the plastic sheet I was lying on and I kept my head down so I wouldn't bump it.

"We need a son-in-law around here. I'm getting too old for this sort of thing," he said as I stood up and took off the old oilskin coat.

I playfully punched him on the arm. "I wouldn't go talking about sons-in-law around Louise these days," I said, looking around to make sure my sister wasn't close by. "Besides, I didn't exactly see you getting your hands greasy."

"It might look like that, but I was in charge and I was responsible," he threw back at me.

I had to laugh—my Dad was actually joking with me. A shadow passed over my heart, too, for all the good times we must have missed with him not being able to hear.

"You know, baby doll, you deserve a treat for doing that nasty job. How about a movie? It's Saturday night, isn't it? Let's see what your old hangdog of a sister thinks of putting down her book and driving us over around the bay."

Amazing grace! Louise thought going to the movie was a fine idea. Dad checked it out with Mother, and she said that if we came home right after the show, she'd manage. That's not what she would have told Louise or me, but never mind. Dad could be charming.

We were giddy in the dory going over to the car. Our gold chariot waited on the shore. Louise drove so fast that if our Sergeant Fletcher had seen her, he would have had to arrest her.

Now, you've got to understand that the movie theatre was just a hall rigged up off the back of the Legion. There was only ever one movie showing and it changed every couple of weeks. When we pulled into the parking lot, people were streaming into the Legion. Louise and I wrinkled our noses at the poster: *True Grit*, with John Wayne and Glen Campbell. Neither of us liked westerns, but we joined the rush anyway, prepared to enjoy a night out whatever was showing. Dad decided to pass on the movie, said he only liked war films, and went into the Legion for a few beers.

The movie hall was dark already, but Louise and I found seats halfway up, in the middle. A couple of kids turned around to say hello to me and took one look at Louise and got up and moved. They were two boys from the hockey team, and I couldn't blame them for not wanting to watch the movie with their principal breathing down their necks.

When my eyes adjusted, I saw that Wish was sitting a few rows away. I was hurt. Why didn't he say he was coming to the show? He could have come with us. I let my eyes drift in his direction again and saw that he wasn't alone. He was sitting beside Beryl. You could pick her out anywhere with her long blonde hair. Louise saw where I was looking and she reached out a hand and touched my arm. I brushed her off and stared straight ahead so she wouldn't see a silly tear splash down my face.

I left before the lights came up, before Wish and Beryl saw me. I walked quickly to the car and slid down into the back seat. Louise went into the bar section of the Legion to get Dad, and every car had left the parking lot and I was shivering before she and Dad came out. There was someone with them, walking toward the car. As they got closer, I saw that it was Sergeant Paul. He was behind Louise, who was walking at a trot. He surged ahead of her, came around to the driver's door and opened it for her to slip in.

"Be careful driving. Moose wander out on the road even at this time of the year," he said before he clicked the door shut for her. She just had time to say, "I know all about the moose, thank you." Dad waved to Paul as Louise backed out of her spot, spun her wheels onto the road and threw rocks and dirt every which way.

"He's quite the young man. Came up to me in the Legion and introduced himself," Dad said.

"He's not a young man, Dad. Has to be close to forty," said Louise as she adjusted her mirror.

"That's young to me, little Miss Sassy," Dad said, using the name he called Louise when she was a child. "He said he thought I had to be your dad, Louise. Said he could see the family resemblance. Said he expected to hear any day about some award you two might get. What's that all about?"

Louise turned her head to catch my eye. Neither of us had thought to tell Dad the story of the rescue. Of course, in the past it would have been too much trouble. Louise wrote to him with the family news every month, and sometimes he sent us a postcard from the *Leif Eiriksson,* the boat his crew worked on. She had probably simply forgotten about the rescue, because she told me many times that her letters were mostly about Mother and the weather and the fishing and hunting.

Louise told him the whole story in about four sentences. He was impressed. "My little girls did that! Wow!" Louise and I rolled our eyes at the "little girls" bit. Then he turned around to me. "Now why is my baby doll so sad? Out with it—did the movie have a sad ending?"

"Leave her alone, Dad. Issy's got teenage-girl troubles and teasing doesn't help."

I said a silent thank you to Louise. She was a better sister than I gave her credit for.

Later, back at the house, Dad said he wanted a cup of our newfangled coffee. I could see that Louise was tired, so I offered to make it for him.

It was only then, when we were alone in the comfort of our kitchen, that I was finally able to tell Dad my troubles. Not about Wish—I would never tell a soul about that. But about my eyes and my reading and the surgery being more than six months away, and about getting sixty in my history test and how I got headaches and that if I had the operation, maybe I could pass grade nine. And once he understood the problem, it turned out he had a friend who might be able to help.

And that's how the doctor marrying Shirley Cameron, which forced the Petersons to scale back on their store, and in turn made Louise buy the car so we could get our groceries, and then Dad coming home to help her pick it out was an unstoppable chain of events that was like a steam train coming down the track toward my new life.

CHAPTER NINE

*Garden party: a communal social gathering held each
summer on grounds surrounding the local church or
another field at which games and contests are held, food
served and funds raised for parish activities*

D
ad got on the phone on Monday morning and called his
doctor friend in Nova Scotia, the one who sent him to the
specialist for his hearing.

"You were so good getting me fixed up, Doctor, I'm wondering
if you can help me again?" he said, layering on the flattery. I could
only hear Dad's side of the conversation, but it wasn't hard to tell
what was going on. "Only if it's no trouble, Doctor. I'd really
appreciate it if you could make some calls to the hospital in Grand
Falls. I remember you told me you knew some people there. My
little girl has had a hard time of it and she's real smart. Getting the
operation done this spring would mean so much to her. Thanks,
Dr. Tulk. We'll sit by the phone and wait to hear."

He winked at me as he hung up with a sweep of his hand,
showing off a bit that he had such influence. "That should do

the trick. Dr. Tulk is one of those guys who knows how to make things happen."

I went to school late because I wanted to hear the phone call. I had a note from Dad, and Miss Simms raised her eyebrows when I handed it to her. I hadn't given the teachers a note in years. Usually I just came and went as I pleased; they could always take it up with the principal.

When the bell rang that day, Miss Simms called me to her desk. She waited to speak until all the other kids had left the room.

"You did very well on that geography quiz last week, Issy. I'm very pleased. A few more quizzes like that one and the history quiz and you could pass this grade. I want you to know that if you need any extra help, I'll be happy to stay after school."

I gave her a searching look. Every teacher in the school had made the same offer to me at one time or another. I rebuffed them all. But I knew the time had come to change. No way was I going to let Beryl Peterson help me ever again.

I had known Beryl was after Wish from the beginning. I knew that was part of the plan, and I had gone along with it. But after seeing them together at the movie, something inside me snapped and I couldn't stand it anymore.

"Yes, Miss," I said and then stood there shifting my weight, trying to find the words to tell her that I couldn't be treasurer of the graduation committee.

But Miss Simms was looking behind me. "What in heavens!" We both turned toward the door to see one of Mildred's little brothers standing there with blood dripping from his nose.

As it turned out, I didn't see Miss Simms for a week after that. By the time I got home from school after helping with little Jimmy and taking him to his sister, everything was settled. The hospital in Grand Falls had called to say that a spot had opened up the very next afternoon for my surgery. I hardly had time to find clean underwear and a nightdress. Dad and I would have to leave at the crack of dawn to drive to Grand Falls, because I had to be there at least two hours before the operation, and I was told not to eat or drink anything for twenty-four hours. Well, we barely had twenty-four hours!

I needn't have worried about the underwear—I soon found out that you don't wear any when you have surgery. The doctor had a quick word with Dad, and he told him that he could fix the seeing problem. "Can't believe the surgery wasn't done when she was a baby. Didn't anyone notice the child was almost blind?" asked the doctor, not really expecting an answer. He took a few minutes to explain to Dad and me how, with my left pupil out of alignment, focusing was difficult because the right eye and left eye couldn't agree on what to look at. He said in some cases it affected distance vision, and in a few rare cases, like mine, it affected close-up vision. Then he said he would also try his hand at the droopy eyelid, but he wasn't making any promises.

"What droopy eyelid?" asked my father. I couldn't tell if Dad was kidding or not. Surely he must have noticed how my eyelid sagged so my left eye looked permanently half closed. I'd been teased about it all my life. The doctor and I looked at each other behind Dad's back. The doctor smiled and again said that he would do his best.

You could tell that the nurses thought Dad was a hunk, it was "Yes, Mr. Heffernan" everywhere we went and "Can I get you a coffee while you're waiting, sir?" It was a real pleasure to see Dad socializing. He used to not speak very much to anyone. He would always smile and show his perfect white teeth, and that made up for a lot, but seeing him chat back and forth with people was a whole new, wonderful experience.

They shook me awake on Wednesday morning, but I wasn't in a good mood about it and I have a vague memory of the nurses having to call my father to tell me to be good. And my wrists were sore; I have another memory of being tied down for a spell.

A light gauze bandage was taped around my eye. Under it my face felt like hot tar was sticking to it, and when I put up my hand to lightly touch where it hurt, I felt a bump as big as a chicken egg.

"Don't touch," said a nurse's voice from somewhere near the foot of my bed.

It was too painful to open my bad eye to see her, and my good eye, the one that had not been operated on, wouldn't open on its own. I fell back onto my pillows.

"I sent your father to have breakfast. He's been here all night giving us a hand. You kept tearing at your eye and your dad helped the night nurse put a straitjacket on you for a couple of hours. You must be exhausted from all your struggling. Pop open your mouth. That's a love. One big fat painkiller that will knock you out for the rest of the day. Cheerio."

The room was dark when I finally came round on Wednesday evening.

"Hello, baby doll," said Dad. "You had a hell of a night. Had us all running for cover."

"Thanks, Dad," I tried to say, but my mouth felt like it was full of cotton wool.

"The doctor's been around a couple of times. Says the operation was a complete success." The way I felt, I didn't care.

"Here's the pretty nurse. She's from down the coast too. Not far from St. Albert's. She's going to help you to the bathroom." I couldn't believe they wanted me to get out of bed. Then I felt a wave of nausea and was out of bed in a heartbeat. I had nausea and dry heaves the rest of the night. I couldn't believe I had willingly come to Grand Falls to let someone hurt me this bad.

Thursday morning, the pain moved from sharp to dull, and I did not feel the need to throw up my guts anymore. Dad was right there reading a newspaper when I woke up. I could see his long shape, which meant my eyes must be open, I thought.

"I'm hungry," I said as I reached out my hand, groping for my glasses. The doctor had explained before the operation that my distance vision wouldn't be any sharper, and that I would need my glasses just the same as before for seeing things far away.

"Wonderful. We've got jelly and we've got cold toast. Breakfast was an hour ago. You do like to sleep, don't you? Guess who's going home today?" said Dad more cheerfully than I needed to hear as he put my glasses on my face, very gently, over the bandage.

I reached out and grabbed his sleeve. "Don't leave me here," I gasped.

"Wouldn't dream of it, baby. The doctor says he needs to see you sometime this morning and if all is well, as he expects it will be, you can get dressed and we're out of here. Now, I don't think you should look in the mirror, but when you're ready we should go for a walk down the hall a bit so you can get your sea legs."

I hurt from the neck up, but I swung my legs out over the bed and found that the rest of me felt pretty good. I just had to get my head to follow my body. Dad put out his arm for me to lean on, and it wasn't long before I was indeed practically jogging along the hospital corridor.

The doctor came in at eleven-thirty, ripped off the bandage and half of my face, or so it felt, looked into my eye with his little flashlight, and handed me a bit of paper and asked me to examine it. I couldn't see the words and was about to cry bitter tears when he told me to put on a pair of glasses he took from his pocket. "Now, try reading the paper with these on."

I looked down and wanted to cry again—this time for all the lost years of my life. Yes, I could see the letters and the words as plain as if they were six inches tall. I didn't have to say anything to the doctor—he knew. He put out his hand, patted me on my shoulder and said, "You'll be just fine now, my dear."

Then he gave Dad a box of white gauze patches and told him that the glasses he'd given me would do for a little while but that I would have to come back in a few weeks for a thorough checkup on the eye. At that time, I would be fitted for contact lenses and glasses for backup. "The swelling will go down in a few days and the bruising will be gone in a week. Patch the good eye every day for six hours to force the old lazy eye to do its job," the doctor said, and then he took my face in his hands and turned me toward the light. "I believe the plastic surgery on the lid was a success too, but we won't know that for sure until all the swelling has disappeared."

Dad had my little overnight bag already packed. "Put on your jeans and sweater, Issy, and let's blow out of this town."

CHAPTER TEN

Nipper: a large biting mosquito

"I hope you're not planning to enter any beauty contests," were the first words out of my sister's mouth when I walked in the door.

Though she smiled and meant it as a joke, Dad shot her a hard look. "I'm sure she'll get enough of that at school. She doesn't need it at home," he said as he helped me find a kitchen chair.

School? Did my father say school? I had no intention of going to school until every trace of bruising had disappeared. I vowed I would not wear an eye patch outside the house. What I desperately wanted to do was have a shower.

I got up to go down the hall and Dad was right on my heel. Give it up already, I thought. "Dad, I can go to the bathroom. I know where I'm going," I said as I gently brushed his hand off my arm.

As soon as I turned on the shower, he was knocking on the door. "The doctor said you can't get your stitches wet. Do you need a hand?" Dad said through the door.

"Go away, I can manage," I said through clenched teeth. I wasn't used to all this attention.

"Unlock the door, Issy, before you get in the shower. If you fall or anything, we need to be able to come in."

Jesus, Mary and Joseph, I thought, just leave me alone. "Don't you dare come in here," I said as I clicked the lock open.

The next moment, Louise was at the door. "I'm going to hand you one of Mother's shower caps. I won't look." And with that, a big fluffy plastic thing was pushed through the door. "Pull it down over your eyes," she said. What a production!

I found my way to the bedroom and flopped down. I was all pooped out. I raised my head, sensing something was different.

Louise came in then with a tray of toast and, guess what, Jell-O!

"Where's Bush?" I asked her. It was very odd that he wasn't chasing after me. We had never been apart before.

"Well, my dear, that's a whole other story," said Louise as she expertly put down the tray. "He put up a racket after you left, barked all night and all the next morning. People must have thought we were beating him. Mother was starting to get hysterical. Wish heard him putting up a racket when he was going by the house, and came in and asked if he could take Bush home while you were away. Bush went with him like a little lamb. Wish was surprised to hear you'd gone to the hospital. I was surprised you hadn't told him," she said, all the while fiddling with the little teapot on the tray.

"Can you phone Wish and ask him to bring my dog back?"

"I'll see if I have time," she said as she straightened some of my clothes piled on a chair. "I've got a lot of do with Dad home for another two days. I can't see why you can't call him yourself."

Over my dead body, I thought.

Oh, but I missed Bush's warmth and his big brown eyes and the thumping of his tail. I managed to get to sleep without him, but I knew I'd have to do something the next day.

I needn't have worried about a thing. Word went around Riverbank as fast as a stampeding caribou that I was back and resting well after very difficult surgery that lasted for hours and hours. I knew that was the story, because Wish brought me a box of Pot of Gold dark chocolates and another Cherry Blossom when he brought Bush back that evening. Louise was gone up to the school and Dad was in the kitchen when Wish and Bush came to the door.

"I heard she had a rare eye disease and the doctors worked on her for a long time," I heard him telling my father with what sounded like real concern in his voice, while Bush came hurtling down the hallway.

My father just laughed. "You know nobody gets anything right around here," he said. Bush was nuzzling my neck when I heard Dad's footsteps coming toward the bedroom. "Sure you can see her, Wish, my boy. I'll just check to see if she's decent."

I dived under the blankets and then poked out my nose and mouth so I could breathe. "Too sick. Can't see anyone," I said in a small, weak voice and managed a few coughs at the same time. No way was I going to let Wish see me looking this awful.

Wish must have left, because Dad came in then and sat on Louise's bed. "That was bad manners, Issy. I thought you had grown up a bit. You and Wish have been friends for a long time. Friends want to help you when you're down, and you've got to let them."

He didn't wait for an answer but got up and left me to my own miserable thoughts. Later, when Beryl dropped in, I made an effort to be civil, though it was one of the hardest things I ever had to do.

"When do you think you'll be well enough to get back to your studying?" she wanted to know. Never, was what I wanted to answer, but I remembered Dad's words and held my tongue. "Miss Simms says that when you're up to it she'll put together some special lessons for you. She didn't say this in front of the class, Issy, just to me.

"We had a meeting about raising money for the graduation. We're going to have a cookie sale just before Easter and we're looking for something to raffle off. The girls want to wear white dresses. Molly Johnson saw a show on TV where the girls all wore white and she's got everyone convinced it's the only way to go. I'm concerned the whole thing is getting out of hand. Not all the girls can afford a new dress, let alone a white dress they may never wear again.

"I've done some adding up and I think we need to raise at least a hundred dollars for decorations and flowers. You know it is always the senior clan that has to raise the money for the graduation. If we do the white dresses, the girls want to wear corsages of red sweetheart roses. I checked and they cost five dollars each, and there are eight girls, and the boys will need to wear boutonnieres at three dollars each, for a total of fifty-eight dollars. And someone has to go to Grand Falls to get them, and—"

"Stop," I said, not able to give Beryl the cold shoulder any longer. "What's this all about? What's a boutonniere? I thought the only money we raised was for some crepe paper and balloons."

"Well, the girls want something different this year. Didn't you hear me? Molly said that on the show she saw, the girls carried small bouquets of flowers. I got them to agree to the corsages, because I knew they would be cheaper. A boutonniere is a little flower a boy wears on his suit jacket so everyone matches. You must have seen Mr. Trudeau with a flower in his jacket lapel?

"I am worried about the dresses, though. Three of the families are on welfare," said Beryl, always the one to worry about the underdogs.

"We could organize a sewing bee," I suggested. "Get a simple pattern. We could add our own touches later to make them look different. There's not much fabric in dresses these days. They would be good for dances next year at the high school, too." The idea had struck me as Beryl was talking.

"And," said Beryl, "they'll be great this summer when it's our turn to work in the stalls at the church garden party." Her eyes lit up. "Why, Issy, that's a wonderful idea. If we make them together, there'll be no competition about who has the best dress. You're brilliant!" She got up from Louise's bed and gave me a big bear hug. Yuck, I thought, but I didn't say a word and let her hug me for three seconds.

"We need to order the pattern and material from the catalogue soon to make sure there's time to do the sewing," I said. I'd never done any sewing, but I'd seen Mother and Louise and Lady doing all kinds and it didn't look all that hard.

"Shoes! What are we going to do about white shoes? No one can afford white shoes unless they're getting married," said Beryl.

I thought for a moment. "White paint. I bet all the girls can come up with a pair of old shoes that fit. We can paint them white. Someone must have leftover white paint."

"Another great idea," said Beryl, and this time I was quick to change the subject before she grabbed me for another hug.

As she was leaving, she said, "This is going to be a lot of fun, Issy. Get well soon so we can start on our plans." Before the porch door banged shut, I could hear her telling Louise that I had some great ideas for the graduation ceremony.

In all the fuss about the dresses and shoes, I had managed to steer Beryl away from the raffle prize. It was usually a special hand-worked cushion or crocheted blanket. I knew I could get a couple of those from Mrs. John. However, the favourite raffle item was a cake. Not just any cake, but one decorated to look like a doll or a dragon or a butterfly. It just so happened that Louise was the queen of cakes. They were what we contributed to raffles, fundraisers and church socials. Because I always helped her with her creations, I knew how to do them too. Should I offer to make one? I wondered. I wasn't sure I was ready for more hugs, so I had decided to think about it a bit.

By the end of the weekend, the swelling around my eye had gone down and the bruising was only a faint yellow tinge. I no longer looked like I'd been attacked by a swarm of nippers. The six hours of eye-patching each day was fine too, I could do it myself, and the tape didn't rip my face. Dad went back to work on Sunday afternoon after telling me that whatever the doctor had done to my eyelid, I was more beautiful than ever. I knew that was the dad in him talking, but he got the smile out of me that he was bent on having before leaving. He hinted this time that, since there was a car around, he might make it home more often.

Louise and I looked at each other over his shoulder. It wasn't only the car that had made this visit different. Mother hadn't whined as much, and Dad had made all her meals for her the last couple of days and sat with her while she ate. We had heard the tinkle of comfortable talk coming from Mother's room.

If someone had told me there would come a day when I looked forward to going to school, I would never have believed her. But that's what happened. I decided the patching could be done entirely in the evenings. I was so bored that school looked positively inviting.

I SPENT A FULL HOUR in front of the mirror before going to school. I got up early because I wanted to take a good hard look and decide for myself if the operation on my droopy eyelid had been a success or not. So far, neither Louise nor my mother had said anything about my left eye, and Beryl hadn't mentioned it during her visit. I wondered if there was something they didn't want to say. The only good mirror with natural light coming in from behind was in the bathroom. I went in and locked the door.

First I checked to see how wide I could open my eye and if my left eye opened as wide as my right one. The eyelid was still a little puffy but not enough that anyone but me could tell. I arched my eyes, popped them, widened them, and looked to the far right and then to the left and up and down. The lid followed every move, though it hurt a little when I shot my eyebrows up to my hairline.

I put on my old glasses and checked the *Reader's Digest* beside the toilet. The words were better than before but still blurry. Looking out the window, I could see as far in the distance as I had before the operation. Then I took out the glasses the doctor had loaned me and picked up the magazine again. I could see everything—the letters, the words, the detail in the drawings, the page numbers. I didn't have to tilt the magazine or my head. I couldn't believe this was what other kids had been seeing all their lives. I looked out the window again and noticed that my distance vision was also sharp with the new glasses. The doctor had already told me that he'd only changed the prescription slightly but that now my two eyes were focusing together.

I took another quick look at my long face with its golden hazel eyes and clear complexion, at my height and my new figure, now down ten pounds, and wondered about what Dad had said on the drive back from Grand Falls. Now that I had tidied up a bit, he said, he could see that I was the spitting image of my mother.

That wasn't something I especially wanted to hear. Maybe lots of girls were thrilled to be told they looked like their mothers, but not me. I had Dad's eye colour, but until my operation and my mother's weight loss I hadn't noticed that I had inherited the oval shape of her eyes, her little hilly nose and long jaw. And her skin. Despite everything, Mother was an English rose, with red-gold hair and unblemished, rosy white skin. I had dark hair, but my skin was as pale and perfect as my mother's. Porcelain is what I heard people call it. My teeth were like hers too, white and square. We were probably exactly the same height, five foot eight. Of course, when she was large you didn't notice that she was tall for a woman, but now that she was down thirty pounds she was starting to carry her height.

Dad had seen the frown on my face when he said I was like Mother. "She was a beauty, you know. The night I met her, she walked into the dance club and every head turned to look at her," he said, patting my shoulder. "You could do a lot worse than look like your mother."

My eye was hurting at the time and all I could do was lie down in the back seat and not move a muscle. We had a two-hour drive ahead of us.

"Tell me about her, Dad," I said. "What was she like before I came along?" I stopped short of saying "and ruined her life," because I wasn't so sure that I had after talking to Louise.

"You didn't ruin her life, baby doll, if that's what you're thinking. She wasn't well long before you came along."

I sat up on my elbow. I didn't know he could read my mind.

"Where do I start? I graduated from high school in Newfoundland with some of the best marks ever seen. Even though there was no money to send me to university, no one in the family wanted me to be a fisherman. Aunt Lady took a year to teach me some bookkeeping skills and then suggested I go to England. Even though it was the Great Depression, she and Dad put together some money for me to get started there in 1936. I worked my passage on a cargo boat. Aunt Lady also gave me letters of introduction to some of her old friends that she'd stayed in touch with, and pretty soon I had a job as a company junior secretary. I was invited to a lot of upper-crust parties and dinners. I had to borrow an evening jacket, but no one seemed to notice I had no money.

"I met your mother at the Florida Club, the year she was a debutante. I hardly knew what a debutante was at the time, but I soon learned the ropes. It's when young girls enter society for the first time and are supposed to find good husbands.

"Agnes was just out of school when we met. She was taking the year to do the round of debutante parties and planning to study French and German. I fell for her that very first time I saw her. So did every other man at the club. She floated through the crowd wearing a pretty yellow dress with splashes of roses, and she had a yellow rose with a pink centre in her red-gold hair.

"She danced with everyone who asked her, and when I saw she wasn't being picky or stuck-up, I got in line. It was like dancing with a butterfly. She wouldn't let me see her home that night, or the next time she came to the club either.

"Then I got lucky. I found out that her father sent a car to pick her up after the dances. One night the driver didn't show up on time and I said I would wait with her. His car had broken down and he was two hours late. She was so grateful I stayed with her that she let me take her to the films the next Sunday afternoon.

"That was in the late spring of 1936. We got married in secret at the end of the summer, before her parents could send her to France and Germany for her studies. Her family made it clear they didn't approve of her marrying outside of their circle. Getting married back then was the only way for us to be together. This wasn't the seventies, remember. Things have changed a lot since your mother and I went out together.

"Less than a year after our very quiet wedding, Louise came along. There were rumbles of war all over Europe and soon I was in a uniform, and before Louise was three your mother was working as a foreman at a factory making bombs. They had a daycare and she could take Louise there with her. She was also head of a local Red Cross committee.

"I never met her family. They cut Agnes off without a word. They never asked about Louise. I don't think they even knew their daughter's married name.

"By early 1943 your mother had seen too many bombs, had gone to too many funerals, and was tired of running into people who asked her about her family. She got very down. So when I suggested she go to Newfoundland with Louise and wait for me there, she jumped at the chance to get away from sirens and ration books. She liked St. John's. She was invited to a lot of teas and socials and evening suppers, and became a leader in raising money for the war effort.

"Then the war was over and I came home, and we moved to Halifax while I went to engineering school. She liked Halifax too, and she'd often take Louise down to the docks to see what ships were coming and going to Southampton.

"Then my father died, and my mother and Aunt Lady needed me here in Riverbank. I never meant to settle back here. After seeing a lot of the world during the war, Riverbank was just too small for me. But I came back, got a job helping to build the power plant. We built the house and I thought Agnes was happy enough. Up until then she'd shown she could adjust to whatever came along. But when I went on the coastal steamers I wasn't around much, and I didn't see the little signs that she was turning into a very unhappy woman. I also didn't know all the work Louise had to do to keep her together. Learning of her parents' death was a real blow.

"It wasn't until you were born that everything really fell apart for good. Agnes had the heart attack, and then went into a deep depression, and after that developed a fear called agoraphobia."

"What?" I asked, showing my surprise.

"For most of the last fifteen years, your mother has had an over-powering fear of going outside. Even leaving her room can be a crisis," he explained. Now why didn't I know this? I bet everyone in Riverbank knew my mother was a mental case.

"That David McKay says there are new methods being developed to treat Mother's kind of illness. He says it's not surprising that someone who lived through bombing raids, and whose parents were killed by an old bomb buried in their own backyard, would develop this fear, especially with a constant threat of nuclear attack."

Even I remembered the Cuban Missile Crisis and had had nightmares about it. I was seven at the time and we were all pretty scared. The teachers had us practise drills at the school and people were stocking up on canned food. Everyone was talking about the Russians and the Americans, the atomic bomb and the Iron Curtain. One day Mother met me and Louise at the door and I started to cry, knowing right then that we were all going to die. Mother told me to smarten up, that the crisis was over, the Russians had pulled back. Then, a year later, President Kennedy was killed and I stayed home watching TV with Mother. She said the Russians did it and I got frightened all over again.

So yes, in a way, I could understand why Mother had this fear.

"And her only brother going missing," added Dad.

"What?!" This was the first time I'd ever heard my mother had a brother.

"I never met him myself. He was younger. She found out from a family servant she ran into one day in Piccadilly—a street in

London—that he joined the navy in 1942. She saw his name on a list in 1944 as missing in action somewhere in the North Atlantic. She never talks about him, but I know it must hurt."

So that's my mother, I thought. She had certainly had a hard life. I had no idea. I wondered to myself why Louise had never told me any of this when I was younger. Now I understood why so many people in Riverbank looked at me with pity in their eyes whenever my mother's name came up. I'd always thought it was because they believed she was too hard on us, but now I realized it was because they knew she couldn't help herself and that she might never get well.

It was the first long conversation I'd ever had with my father. I suspected that his own life of silence and absences hadn't helped Mother. He was the only person her own age in her life and he was seldom home, and when he was home his hearing loss must have been a real problem. Suddenly and for only a second, my father's many charms disappeared, and I saw a weak man who abandoned his wife and kids when he could have been home working at a good job and being a husband and a dad.

"Do you think you'll ever get a job closer to home?" I blurted out. For a shining moment I had this picture in my head of Louise and me getting on with our lives and Dad and Mother holding hands as they sat side by side in rocking chairs on the wide front veranda. (Never mind that we didn't have a front veranda.)

"I'm chief engineer now for all the government ferries in Atlantic Canada, baby doll. I can't see what kind of job I could do down here anymore that would be as interesting. And I like working on the water, though I must admit that more and more I spend most of my days in my office in North Sydney. I used to have a cabin on one of the ferries, but I gave that up because I never use it anymore. They added a little apartment to my office so I can be on call at all hours."

"Buy a boat," I muttered under my breath.

One night a few days later, when the lights were out, I asked my sister why she had never told me the whole dark story about Mother's illness.

"I was going to, when you turned sixteen. I didn't think you could understand. I didn't want to burden you with it."

My little talk with Dad helped me to see Mother differently. I wasn't quite so snarly if she said she couldn't come out to the kitchen just then for her tea. I understood better why Louise went through hoops not to upset Mother and spent so much time with her in the evening, helping her to get to sleep. I understood why the doctor came across the water to her and didn't insist she come to his clinic. Mostly, I understood that it took a lot of effort to make Mother feel safe. And I began to understand why there had been so little time for me over the years.

CHAPTER ELEVEN

Odds: difference, consequences,
esp. in phrase "what odds?"

A week back at school showed that I still had masses of work to do. The words were laid out before me, both on the pages and on the blackboard, but I found there were far too many to learn. Thanks to Beryl's and Louise's work, I knew how to print and could put a lot of simple words together. But no matter how I tried, I couldn't turn many of the sounds I heard into the written word. The word *vehicle* put me in a tizzy, and a word like, well, *possible* was impossible. And who would have thought that *ph* sounded like *f*? And apparently there were rules about using even some of the simple words. I couldn't tell the difference between: *write* and *right, there* and *their, of* and *off, hear* and *here.* I had none of the foundation that the other students in my grade had built up over the years.

I did try. I put my heart back into it and worked with the teacher after school, and Louise stepped in to guide me on the weekends. She was a lot more patient this time, now that she understood I wasn't deliberately being stupid and that I had a lot of catching up to do.

All the while I was treasurer of the graduation committee, and that was taking up more time than I ever imagined.

The girls in the class met after school and went through the catalogue and agreed on a pattern and a fabric for the dresses. Beryl and I tried to steer them toward basic broadcloth, the cheapest fabric available. But some of the girls were sewers themselves and thought broadcloth was so cheap it was a waste of our time; they said none of us would ever wear the dresses again. Diane Smith read the small print in the catalogues and discovered that if we purchased more than ten yards of any one fabric, there was an automatic 20 percent discount in Sears, even if the fabric was already on sale. So we spent a good deal of time daydreaming about the chiffon, the tulle, the satin and the silk and then looked at the sale pages. We agreed that the polyester organza would work out to almost the same price as the broadcloth with the discount, and Molly Johnson said that if we lined the organza with white acetate, we'd have fairly nice dresses. They got excited when Beryl pointed out that, with the addition of a bit of embroidery or a coloured ribbon or two, they'd look good for the summer garden party or for a dance over at the high school next year. Being thrifty was part of our upbringing.

The pattern looked dead simple and came with three different necklines and three different sleeves. Again, Molly pointed out that if we combined different necklines and sleeves, the dresses would hardly look alike at all but would be similar enough for the graduation to make it seem as if we'd planned it all. It made sense. They got a real laugh out of my idea of painting shoes, but we agreed that if we all did it, it would work. In other words, no one was to go out and get new white shoes and shame the rest of us. I didn't have to say much at any of these meetings. Nothing was expected of me except a nod occasionally to let them know I agreed.

We made plans for our first fundraiser, the cookie sale, for the week after Easter. The school was having its first spring bingo, so the timing was perfect. The girls in my class tried to convince me to lead the Easter parade in a blue dress and white veil, carrying paper lilies kept in the church basement, but I managed to get out of it by saying my mother needed me. I couldn't believe they had asked me, because the girl who played the Virgin Mary was always one of the prettier girls in the school. She also had to be able to wear a size ten dress!

I was very pleased that we sold a good selection of cookies, fudge and homemade candy and made $22.43. I kept the money in a little box on the dresser in my bedroom and counted it every day just to be sure.

At the end of April, the hospital called to say I had the follow-up appointment for my eye. Now this was a problem because, while I was set to run away to Toronto in June all by myself, I didn't exactly feel comfortable going to Grand Falls on my own, and Louise couldn't take another day off school.

Then, as luck would have it, Beryl let it slip that Wish had to take his granddad to Grand Falls for medical tests the same day I had to go. I didn't say anything because I was scared to travel in the same car as Wish's granddad, but soon enough Beryl put two and two together and figured out how to make it work.

"The Captain is very sick, Issy, and if you pull a hat down over your eyes and don't say a word until he falls asleep, he won't know there's a Heffernan in the car. I'll phone Wish and see what he thinks." That's what she did and she got it all sorted out.

Wish was especially keen to make the plan work because Louise was willing to lend him her car if he took me with him. We set off at first light, back up the dirt road to civilization.

I was shocked to see how frail Wish's granddad had become. Wish practically lifted him up in his arms to put him in the dory, and then lifted him out of the dory, supported him up the path to the car and wrapped him in a heavy blanket against the chill of the morning air off the river. I slouched down in the front seat until Wish had his grandfather settled in the back. Mr. Sweetapple didn't give me a second glance. Very soon he was breathing lightly and fast asleep.

I didn't know what to say to Wish. We drove in silence for a few minutes. I used to like being quiet, saying nothing, not having anyone bother me, but this silence was painful. An unbidden tear splashed down my face. I looked out the window right away, but Wish saw me wipe away the big, glistening drop.

"What's wrong, Issy?" he asked in a voice as soft as velvet. I didn't want to say anything, but there was something wrong, and this time I wanted to speak about it rather than sulk.

"Wish, I feel so bad. I had no idea that your granddad was so sick. I didn't know that was what was making you so sad."

His hand reached across the seat and took hold of mine. "It's okay, Issy. You were busy too, what with your operation and catching up at school."

I think if he hadn't been touching me, I would have been very angry with him. My problems at school were my secret. If I passed grade nine like everyone else, he might never learn how backward I was, how hard I had been pushing myself. That's what I thought, anyway, but then I remembered how there are no secrets in small towns.

"You know what makes me sad, Issy?" he asked.

I sniffled but still didn't look at him, though I was praying he would leave his hand covering mine for a million years.

"I thought we were friends. I thought you could trust me. I had to find out about all your troubles from Beryl. You could have told me yourself and I would have been so happy to help you out," he said, keeping his eyes on the road.

That's when my one tear became a torrent. I found a Kleenex in my pocket and blew my nose. I tried to be quiet so as not to wake Mr. Sweetapple. What could I do but tell Wish the truth?

"I didn't want you to know how stupid I was. The teachers always found a way to pass me to the next grade, but I couldn't read. Wish, I couldn't read! I thought I was stupid, maybe even retarded. It held me back in just about everything. And my mother hated me and Louise treated me like a leper, and Dad was never home. I had Lady, thank goodness, and when she died in the winter, I thought mine was the most miserable existence on earth.

"Nobody understood that I couldn't *see* the words on the page until one night when Louise wrote the words big," I said, sniffling and dabbing at the tears that wouldn't stop.

"There, there, Issy. I always knew you were too smart to be stupid. You should have trusted me like you did when you were a kid," he said, reaching out and pulling my chin toward him.

"Can we start again?"

Start what? I wondered, and opened my eyes wide with the question in them.

"Can we be friends like when we were youngsters?" he explained.

I looked at him and smiled a "Yes, of course." What odds? Then I moved ever so carefully an inch toward the car door, just enough so his hand couldn't reach mine very easily. Friends shouldn't be touching that way; even a bumpkin like me knew the difference.

It was a pretty drive into central Newfoundland. The ice was melting in the ponds and dripping off the trees, and the road was bare of snow. Wish took his granddad for his appointments and I went bravely off by myself, slowly and carefully reading signs that pointed me to the right office.

I'd have to come back in a couple of weeks when the contacts came in, but the doctor was delighted with how my vision had improved. He poked around my eyelid for a few seconds and declared the plastic surgery to be an amazing success. I was as happy as a crow in a garbage dump when I met up with Wish at the appointed time and place. He was looking very bleak. My eyes asked what was wrong.

"It's Granddad. They won't let me take him home. They say he should be in hospital, that he hasn't long to …" And with those words he broke down entirely and sobbed. It was my turn to touch him. I put an awkward arm around his shoulder, but he pulled me into his arms and hung on for dear life, right there in the fluorescent-lit green patient lounge.

"Granddad wouldn't want to die in a hospital. I want to bring him home and put his bed in the front room so he can see the river. I can take care of him," Wish sobbed into my ear.

"Won't they listen to you?"

"No, they say I'm too young to understand and to know what's best. How can they say that? He's my granddad and I love him."

I missed a breath and perhaps a heartbeat. The word "love" was never spoken in our house, yet it seemed so natural for Wish to say he loved his grandfather. Of course he did.

"I'll phone Louise. She'll know what to do," I said as I slipped out of his arms and left him looking pitiful, his face buried in his shoulder on an orange moulded-plastic chair.

I had never made a phone call in my life, but I knew I had to do this for Wish. I found a phone booth and looked at the darn thing for a long time. I lifted the handset and wondered how you called long-distance. I saw the little word *Operator* and dialed the zero. A woman with a deep, warm voice answered, "Newfoundland Telephone," and she helped me place a collect call—nothing to it, really—and very soon I was explaining the situation to Louise. She said she would see what she could do. I went back and sat with Wish in the waiting room. We sat for two hours, neither of us hardly moving a muscle.

Finally, a young nurse came out of a set of grey double doors pushing Mr. Sweetapple in a wheelchair. He looked very frail, his skin paper thin and flour white.

"The school principal down your way called. She said she would take full responsibility for your grandfather. She said Dr. McKay will take him on as a patient and we confirmed that with the doctor. The principal sounded like a very fine woman, and we felt your grand-father will be in good hands between her and the doctor." The nurse said all this while wheeling Mr. Sweetapple toward the car. She watched as we got him settled in the back seat, and when she saw how careful Wish was, she leaned into the car and said, "You have a fine grandson, Mr. Sweetapple," and she tucked him up again in such a way that the blanket would not fall off.

It was a quiet ride back to Riverbank. I think Wish was moving his grandfather's bed around in his head, and making plans for calling the doctor, and perhaps thinking about life after his grand-father passed away. I was thinking about poor Mr. Sweetapple too, but I managed to slip in a few moments for the contact lenses I would be getting and for the warm feeling that came over me whenever I was close to Wish. I wondered if there was any way he would let me help him.

Louise knew how bad things were. She was waiting on the wharf with Lolly McKinnon's old wheelchair. Lolly was long dead, but her niece kept the chair for anyone to borrow who needed it.

We were a mournful little group pushing our way along the road to Sweetapple Lane.

I DIDN'T KNOW how to help Wish at first. He was so self-contained. He didn't need help moving furniture, or cleaning the house, or making meals, or sitting with his granddad. No, he was able to do it all.

A few days after our trip to Grand Falls, Louise asked me to go over to Wish's house with a tuna casserole and a crock of beef broth.

"What about the family feud?" I asked.

"What are you going on about?" asked Louise as she wrapped a tea towel around the Pyrex dish.

"Mr. Sweetapple said a while back that all Heffernan women were hussies," I said.

"What a funny thing to say. I'm more than eighteen years older than you and I've never heard of any family fight. Mind you, we've not had much to do with the Sweetapples except for the time when you were a youngster and you tagged along after Wish. Certainly, Lady and Mr. Sweetapple never talked to one another that I can remember—and that is odd, now that you mention it. If there was anything going on, we don't know about it, so it'll end with our generation," she said very matter-of-factly. "Now scoot, before the food gets cold."

I still didn't want to upset Mr. Sweetapple, so I tapped on the kitchen window to get Wish's attention and motioned for him to come outside. Wish looked like he hadn't slept or eaten since we brought the old man home.

"Granddad's in the front room, so come in. He won't know you're here if you're quiet," he said as he took the food out of my arms.

I knew right away that Wish needed to eat, so I turned on the stove to heat up the kettle and made tea. There's nothing like tea in a time of crisis. I smiled when that idea sprung into my head, because they were Mother's words. The kitchen was immaculately clean and tidy. I laid a table in front of the window and put the tuna casserole on a plate and the soup in a large mug.

"Eat," I said to Wish, "now." I hated to be bossy, but I was finding that when I had to, I had the Heffernan knack for it.

He moved toward the food but stopped when he heard his

granddad whimper. "I'll feed him some broth first," he said. He went into the front room, pulled up a chair beside his grandfather and began to spoon-feed him from the mug. I stood in the shadow of the door and watched the two of them. Wish worked hard at it, but scarcely anything was going down. He got about six spoonfuls into his granddad's mouth before his head suddenly fell forward.

"Wish," I whispered, "is your granddad all right?" I was half scared to death.

"Yes, he does that. The doctor says it's his heart. He just blacks out. He's doing it a couple of times a day now."

I didn't know what Wish knew, but it was clear to me that the end was very near. I signalled to Wish to come out to the kitchen.

"Wish, you have to call your aunt and uncle. I know they're not related to your granddad, but they will want to know. Arrangements are going to have to be made soon, and they'll be able to help you with them," I said, trying to get him to see what was coming.

"I can't, don't you see, Issy. If Granddad … if Granddad dies, they'll insist I come back to Toronto right away."

"But Wish, you can't keep something this big from them. Just think how fortunate it was that you came back to be with him. It's possible your grandfather could have died alone, and we might not have noticed for days. He's been pretty much a recluse since your grandmother died and mad at everyone. At least call your great-aunt Effie. She'll want to know about her brother.

"It'll take a while to clear up your grandfather's things, and someone has to be here to do that. You'll probably need the whole summer just for that."

"Issy, my little friend who isn't so little anymore," he said, pulling me to him, "you're right, I need to talk to them. I'll call them later, when Uncle is home from work. I'll phone Great-aunt Effie tonight too. Can you sit with me a bit?"

He finished his supper and then we sat quietly on the daybed in the corner of the kitchen, until the only light was the moonbeams sneaking in through the windows of the front room. I tried not to move, because Wish was soon sound asleep and he needed his rest desperately.

"Yoo-hoo, is there anyone home?" said a voice coming from the direction of the back pathway. Wish and I sprung apart. It was Beryl. "I brought some chocolate cake. Hello, Issy, I'm glad Wish is not here alone. Please wait, Issy, there's enough cake for all of us."

But I was gone, out the door like a shot. For an hour back there, I had forgotten that Beryl and Wish were a couple. I had been happy pretending Wish and I were back in our childhood and the best of friends.

CHAPTER TWELVE

Race: a generation

The girls were going on and on about their dresses and shoes and raising money for the corsages. Mother was coming out to the kitchen more often and sat with Louise and me twice that week to have her supper. She didn't harangue me once, but, that said, I was extra careful not to annoy her, either. Louise asked me about my dress over supper and Mother got very interested in the project.

My heart wasn't in any of it. Wish's aunt had come down from Toronto, and I spent as many hours as I could up in the cemetery, sitting near Lady's grave and watching Wish's house. His great-aunt Effie had come over, too, and while I wanted to visit with her, I knew this was not the time. The doctor was going in and out and there was little doubt the end was very near. My heart was breaking for Wish and all that he was going through.

It was an unbearable sadness and a relief when word went around that Mr. Sweetapple had died peacefully in his sleep, the last of that Sweetapple race.

I thought it would be a quiet funeral up at the church, but once Mr. Higgins-Jones arrived, the funeral was moved to St. Albert's. I learned the reason for this later. Wish had found a medal from World War I in his grandfather's desk drawer and Mr. Higgins-Jones, an amateur military historian, knew it to be the Military Medal, awarded only for great acts of bravery. He made some quick phone calls to military libraries and learned that Mr. Sweetapple, or Captain Aloysius Sweetapple, had indeed risked his life to save six men from certain death on the battlefield in 1917. His Military Medal had been awarded by the King and noted in the *Times* of London. Mr. Higgins-Jones said this meant that Mr. Sweetapple deserved a military funeral with all the honours.

So we all got in boats to cross the river and cars to drive around the bay to the St. Albert's Legion. An honour guard came down from the military base in Gander, and the four RCMP corporals in the bay area put on their red serge and stood with heads bowed at the four corners of the casket. It was quite moving, and when they played "Taps," I had a terrible itch in my eye that wouldn't go away. Wish's granddad was laid to rest in Riverbank, not far from Lady. Wish stood between his aunt and uncle and it was clear that the three of them were not at ease with each other.

I was turning away from the grave, keeping a respectful distance, when I heard my name called. It was Wish.

"Don't leave, Issy. I want you to meet my aunt and uncle," he said as an early May breeze ruffled his long curls.

Meeting new people was difficult for me, but Wish was determined to ignore my anxiety. He stepped toward me, took my arm and gently eased me over to where the Higgins-Joneses stood.

"This is Issy," he said simply.

"Ah, yes, Issy," said Mrs. Higgins-Jones. "We've heard a lot about you." Her wide eyes underneath perfectly plucked brows took in all of me in one long sweep. The way she breathed deep from her nose made it clear she didn't approve.

I wasn't sure if it was my imagination or not, but Wish's uncle appeared to step intentionally between Wish and me so that we were forced to pull apart. And surely he didn't turn his shoulder just slightly so that I was pushed outside the family circle? I had never witnessed such rudeness. I was about to turn and walk away when I felt Wish's hand on my elbow.

"I'm going to walk Issy back to her house," he said, almost daring them to stop him.

"Of course, Alfred," said his aunt while they both took in my cheap black coat from the Sears catalogue and put their noses higher in the air.

His great-aunt Effie noticed me then. "Why, Issy, my dear, you must come back for tea again soon. I've missed you." I felt like hugging her and, heaven forbid, I bent down and did it, right there in front of the Higgins-Joneses. I figured I'd give them something to talk about.

Again I felt Wish's hand on my arm, turning me toward home. This was the first time I was close enough to Wish to talk to him since his grandfather died. I didn't know if I'd ever see him again—if he was leaving that very day, or if it would be tomorrow, or if they were going to allow him to stay for the summer.

The question must have been in my eyes. Wish pulled me close and whispered in my ear, "I'm going to stay until the end of

August." The tension left my body and I smiled, like I'd just got the only present I ever wanted.

"You have beautiful dimples," Wish was saying when his aunt interrupted to remind him to be home within the half-hour. I blushed a deep pink. That's when I looked around to see where Beryl was. The funny thing was, she hadn't come to the service in St. Albert's, and now she wasn't in the cemetery.

Just as Wish was leaving me at my gate, Great-aunt Effie came up behind me with Wish's aunt and uncle. "The next time you come for tea, I want to tell you why my brother was against the Heffernans and Sweetapples ever getting mixed up with each other," she said.

I found my manners and said that I hoped to see her soon, and Mrs. Higgins-Jones gave me a long, searching look.

CHAPTER THIRTEEN

Mamateek: Beothuk winter wigwam

In the middle of May, two weeks after the funeral, two official letters came to the post office—one for me and one for Louise. I opened mine with great care, because letters addressed to me were very scarce. This would in fact be the first time I'd be able to read one. Well, I could read most of it, anyway. Louise had to help me with the big words, and I have to say she was generous about it. Somewhere in the past two months she had stopped using the word "stupid" in connection with me.

It was about the bravery award, and after reading the letter twice I understood that we were going to be awarded a certificate for showing bravery and saving the life of another human being. Louise said it wasn't my fault that I had to read the letter twice to understand it; she said it was written in legal terms and was very poorly composed indeed.

Mother, who was out in the kitchen more often than not now, and who had lost at least forty pounds, was excited—until she realized Louise and I would have to go up the road to Grand Falls yet again. I had been to Grand Falls twice in my life before this winter, and now I was going there for the third time this year, and the year wasn't half over yet.

"How will I manage if you two are off gallivanting around Grand Falls for the day?" she said in a voice that was very close to, but not quite, a whine.

"You'll manage just fine, Mother," said Louise, as my jaw almost dropped off in surprise. "I'll leave you some salads in the fridge. You must remember how to make a cup of tea, and it'll give me a chance to look around the big Co-op up there to see if it has any of those low-calorie cookies we saw advertised in *Chatelaine*," continued this new Louise, who had only ever been a doormat when it came to what Mother wanted.

Mother must have liked the bribe. We normally hid any cookies from her, and ice cream was now banned from our home. If Louise and I wanted ice cream, we had to eat it while we were out. I already had visions of sitting at the Woolworth counter and eating a whopping big banana split with buckets of whipped cream.

"I want the chocolate kind, if they have them, and I want you home before seven. That road is dark and you have to be careful," Mother said, agreeing to the deal and being pretty reasonable about it. I think I even heard a note of concern in her voice.

Of course, we knew to be careful. Every year one or two people from down our way were killed by driving into a moose on the dark highway. Now, if you want stupid, that would be a moose. People said they came to the highways to lick the salt used to melt the snow and ice. If they saw headlights, they ran toward them, not away. They're big animals, most of them over a thousand pounds, so you had to be careful.

A half-hour later, Wish came by to say he too had a letter. It was embarrassing for me, because he was getting a certificate for saving my life. He said the Petersons would be going to the ceremony, because little Rosalie wanted to be there. Of course, he would have dropped by the Petersons' first.

Since his grandfather had died, Wish was spending his time cleaning out the house and fixing it up. He seemed to be having a good time doing it, and was running around asking anyone he could corner for advice on the roof, the windows, the fence and the wiring. He was arranging to ship a couple of old pieces of furniture, which his aunt had been heard to call "antiques," to Toronto, and again he was asking advice all around. He was quite the popular young man. He dropped in home a couple of times and told me that he had turned down the job at the power plant but was going to work on road construction for the summer.

We were expecting an election in the fall, and it looked like the government was going to change after twenty-two years of Joey Smallwood, the premier who changed us from a British colony into a province of Canada. There was some agitation for a bridge to Riverbank, but the pre-election goody we were getting this time was money to widen and pave the dirt road to Grand Falls. Wish would be cutting and burning the roadside brush—hard work, especially in the heat of July and August. In addition to the heat, there would be swarms of nasty little blackflies that took chunks out of your skin and gorged themselves on your blood.

JUST IN THE NICK OF TIME we got a phone call saying my
contact lenses had come in, and Louise arranged for us to leave an
hour earlier than we had planned for the awards ceremony so I
could have my lenses fitted first thing in the morning.

It all went like clockwork. It was a lovely morning, so the boat
ride across the river, often a trial, was magical. There was mist on
the water and I felt like a princess gliding through low-lying
clouds. My lenses fit perfectly the first time, and after some practice taking them out and putting them in, I was ready. The doctor
said I could leave them in for four hours. Then Louise helped me
pick out a pair of glasses for backup, and we actually had some
fun. She talked me into getting brown square frames with a hint of
gold in them. I was very proud of myself for convincing Louise,
without upsetting her, that the black rims she was wearing were
just a bit too heavy for her narrow face, and she splurged on oval
wire frames. With her hair down, she looked more like Joni
Mitchell than Marian the Librarian.

The small hall where the certificates were to be presented was
just across the street, and we had an hour to kill. It was only ten
o'clock in the morning, but I persuaded Louise to take me to
Woolworth's for a banana split. I kept reminding her there was a
lot of nutrition in a banana, and that bananas were a good, healthy
breakfast food. She sat with me at the counter and had a little
metal pot of tea while I attacked the huge dish of ice cream,
whipped cream and chocolate sauce with a red cherry on top.

"You'll put the weight back on if you eat like that," she said.

I didn't care, I was in heaven. Besides, a banana split once or
twice a year wasn't going to put ten pounds back on my bones.

Get a life, I felt like saying, but she wasn't being fussy about letting me come here and paying the bill, so I let it go.

As we walked across the street, I couldn't help but think that five months ago Louise would have had to threaten to rip out my fingernails to get me to come to Grand Falls and go up in front of a group of people to accept an award. My nerves were still shattered, but I knew that with Wish in the room and all the Petersons there as support—yes, even Beryl—my knees would get me to the front of the room. And I figured if I fainted, Louise would be there to catch me. She owed me that, since it was mostly her fault we were here.

In the end, I wasn't the one who was awestruck. Sergeant Fletcher was there in his red serge to help the mayor hand out the awards, and Louise looked at him like a rabbit caught in the headlights. He was fumbling his words a lot more than you'd expect from a police officer who was used to being in charge. When our names were called, I had to nudge Louise to move up to the front of the room with me, and when the sergeant handed over the certificates, hers floated to the floor and I had to chase after it, which got a laugh from everyone in the room.

Six of us were getting awards that day, from south and central Newfoundland, and with our families, and the families of the people whose lives were saved, there was a little crowd at the community centre. Afterwards there was tea and tiny little egg salad sandwiches and yummy cupcakes with lashes of pink, creamy icing—fairy cakes, my mother would have called them.

A woman named Kate Derby, from a St. John's newspaper, talked to Louise and the Petersons about the rescue. I didn't have to say anything, thank goodness, but I was quite taken with Miss Derby. She looked like she had nerves of steel and a heart of ice. She told everyone where to stand for the photos and when to smile, and she didn't mind interrupting the mayor to ask questions. A couple of guys were drawn to her beautiful blue eyes, but she barely noticed anyone unless she was interviewing them, and then she was all ears while she furiously wrote notes. She was the first real career woman I had ever seen, except for the teachers up at the school and the nurses at the hospital. This Kate Derby was a reporter, and she was bossing people around like she owned the place.

Even though we were as different as night and day, I liked her on the spot. I had no trouble talking to her and I soon found out that she grew up in Corner Brook but spent most of her summers in a place called Cook's Cove, which, she said, had been tiny and isolated. It impressed me that she could come from such a place and be a career woman. When she stopped for a moment to change the film in her camera, she noticed the charm bracelet around my wrist.

"It's lovely," she said. "It's one of the prettiest I've ever seen." I blurted out that my mother had one and then I babbled on about how my mother was from England and how she couldn't be here today because she wasn't well and couldn't handle the drive up from Riverbank. I fiddled with Lady's cross then, and Kate noticed that too.

"It's a Celtic gold cross and looks as old as the hills of Ireland," she said as she snapped the back of her camera shut and moved into the crowd to take photographs. I was surprised she could tell so much from such a quick look, and I touched its warmth to remind myself of Lady.

Little Rosalie was as cute as a button, dressed in a Newfoundland green and yellow and red tartan kilt and smiling from ear to ear. She looked fragile but lovely. Her hair was neat, pulled back in what I heard people call a French braid. Her blouse was spotless, and she was taking care of her constant sniffles with a white embroidered lacy handkerchief left over from another world.

Louise was very quiet, except to tell me not to crane my neck as it was rather unattractive. I was looking for Wish, to see who he was with and how he was getting home. I should have known he'd be with the Petersons, and sure enough, he was on the far side of the room with Beryl by his side. He saved my life, he should be with me! I wanted to stamp my foot.

That's when I saw the Petersons move toward us, all seven of them in a bunch, like a school of fish, with Rosalie in the lead. I tried backing into the wall, disappearing into the furniture. There was no doubt they were coming to see me and Louise. Rosalie got to us first, just as excited as a hornet near an open bottle of Coke. I saw she had something in her hands. Mrs. Peterson caught up with her daughter rather breathlessly. "Rosalie wants to say something, Miss Heffernan and Issy, my dear."

"Thank you for saving my life," said the little blue-eyed darling as she handed us each a box that matched her eyes. I'd seen the blue box before, and then I remembered it was from Birks, that expensive place in St. John's where Mother sometimes ordered her charms. I looked to Louise.

"Why, you didn't have to get us anything. This is very kind of you. Thank you, child," she said in her perfect principal voice.

"Open them," commanded Rosalie. And we did. A lovely silver charm for each of us in the shape of an angel.

I looked up and caught Wish's eye. I got so flustered I dropped the darn box, and when he bent to pick it up, he hit me on the chin and I smacked him on the ear. Everyone laughed, but I was so ashamed of myself. I hadn't got Wish a present, yet he had saved my life. He knew what I was thinking and tugged at my sleeve so that I moved out of the crush of the crowd.

"If you remember, you weren't exactly pleased that I saved your life. I left that part out of the report. I figure, since you didn't kill me, we're even," he said with a smile growing in his eyes.

"Come on, Issy, you and I have a job to do," said Beryl. Wish and I were a bit too cozy, you see. But she was right—we had agreed to go to the florist together to see about the corsages and boutonnieres. Graduation was only a month away, and we wanted to know what we would be spending on the flowers.

"Remember, Issy, you have to help me with the groceries," said Louise. "I can pick them up myself, but I'll need help carrying the bags."

Now how did the sergeant hear her say that? He was halfway across the room and Louise hadn't raised her voice.

"I can help you with the bags, Miss Heffernan. I have to pick up a few things at the Co-op myself. Can you wait five minutes while I go to the detachment and change out of my uniform? By the way, congratulations to you and your sister," he said as he closed the gap between himself and Louise. "I have to drop into the library too, but that will only take a second, the librarian has a stack of books waiting for me."

Louise didn't know where to look and finally sputtered out a thank you and a yes, of course, she could wait five minutes.

"Wish, you come with us," ordered Beryl. "We need your advice on what's best for the boys in the class." I wished I had that girl's nerve sometimes.

"We can go over in my car," said Wish. And that's how I found out his aunt and uncle had given him a vehicle, a word I could finally spell.

It was a cute little green two-door Volkswagen Beetle. He proudly showed me the radio and the wipers and how the trunk was in the front and the engine in the back. He talked about gas mileage for a full minute. Beryl was rolling her eyes like she'd been through the demonstration a few times already. I thought it strange that when Wish opened the passenger door, Beryl pushed the seat button and got in the back, leaving the front seat for me.

Beryl managed to get us a discount on the flowers and arranged for them to be delivered on the bus the morning of the graduation. She said we'd prepay with a cheque in a couple of weeks. That meant we'd better get cracking and raise more money.

Then we went over to the Co-op and found that the Petersons were there too. After some confusion we were all in the parking lot, and somehow it came up that some people had things they needed to do in Grand Falls and others had to get home. I remained silent, couldn't have put a word in edgewise if I'd tried. The Peterson kids were clamouring for attention—one wanted ice cream, another french fries, and Rosalie said she had to go to the bathroom. It turned out that Sergeant Fletcher had come up in a police cruiser that was in the garage and wouldn't be ready until Tuesday, and

Wish said something about needing my advice on a suit he was thinking about buying, and Beryl needed to go home to write a letter (now that was one I hadn't heard before). Whew! Then I found myself standing there waving Louise and the sergeant off, and hardly responded when Wish sprinted ahead and opened his passenger door for me. I was dizzy. What had just happened?

"You don't mind, do you, Issy?" he said, half apologizing for bullying me into his car. Well, I was still a little mad at him for playing me off against Beryl, but what the heck, I thought, this time I was just going to enjoy myself.

"Not at all, Wish," I said, looking at his chest, and then I raised my eyes with a flutter to gaze into his. "Not at all."

That's when I remembered it was past the time to take out my contacts. With anyone else I would have been mortified, but when I couldn't blink them out, it was Wish who used the little plunger gadget the doctor had given me to fish them out of my eyes. He was good at stuff like that.

Wish didn't get the suit. He said the cut wasn't right, though it looked great to me. Instead, I followed him around while he got two pairs of jeans and safety boots for his job. I insisted he buy a baseball hat, knowing he would need it once he was working in the sun, and he even went for the red bandana I suggested to put around his neck. We went to the Chinese restaurant for an early supper, and Wish knew exactly what to order.

After that, we walked along the Exploits River, eating double ice cream cones, and Wish told me the story of Shawnadithit, the last Beothuk, who was found almost starving to death around Grand Falls, and about Mary March, another Beothuk, who was one of the last to be captured by the English. He forgot that he had told me the same stories lots of times when we were youngsters. And I certainly didn't tell him we'd learned the stories in school, too, and that I probably knew more about the Beothuk's mamateeks than he did.

Despite all the warnings about moose, I didn't really expect to see one on the drive home. I'd spotted one or two standing on the side of the road a couple of times during drives to St. Albert's. Those times it was daylight and there were no headlights to daze them, so there was lots of time to slow down in case the moose decided to cross the road. This time it was pitch-black, no moon, and we were in a hurry to get home so we wouldn't have to spend the night waiting on the far shore. Wish saw the big bull moose a split second before I did. He jammed his foot on the brakes and we went into a skid across the pavement. I reached out for his arm, closed my eyes and held on tight. We came to a hard stop a mere foot from the edge of the road and a steep gully. Except for the gouge I made with my fingernails in Wish's arm, we seemed to be okay. We were lucky we were both wearing our seat belts.

The moose ever so casually moved away from the centre of the road and walked toward us. He stopped right behind the car. We could hear him chomping and chewing the young grass.

"Now what?" I said in a whisper, not expecting an answer.

"I think we blew a tire. As much as I'd like to drive away from that big guy, I think we have to wait for him to move. If he doesn't, we'll have to put on the spare tire with him watching over us."

We waited, but the moose appeared to have found a succulent bit of green and was taking his time over his bedtime snack. Ten minutes is a long time when you're trapped in your car by a moose.

"I'm getting out," said Wish. Again we were lucky, because the trunk was in the front. Wish moved slowly and talked softly to the moose. "Issy, you're going to have to hold the flashlight while I change the tire," said Wish, again in a calm, reassuring voice.

I opened the car door as quietly as I could. I knew my knees would buckle if the moose as much as looked in my direction, and my hands trembled so hard it was difficult to hold the flashlight steady. Wish kept talking softly, reassuring the moose (and me) that everything was just fine.

Inch by inch we moved back to the car doors. We pulled them closed but didn't bang them. Wish started up the engine, put the car in first gear and slowly eased back onto the road. The moose raised his head and looked around.

"Easy, Wish," I said, "I've heard stories of moose kicking in windows and chasing after cars and outrunning them."

Once again, luck was with us—our moose simply kept on eating. Five miles down the highway we stopped for a moment to pull our doors shut. We didn't say a word the rest of the trip, and when we got to the parking lot Wish pulled me into his arms and buried his face in my hair. I knew then that he'd had a scare too.

"You're the only girl I know who I could depend on not to scream her head off back there," he murmured.

We fit together very nicely, even with a stick shift between us. He was so warm and snugly.

I pulled away. "It's time we got home," I said, though if he'd asked me at that moment, I would not have gone home at all.

By the time we waited for Mr. Jeddore to come across for us, it was well past midnight before I inched open the porch door. I turned to Wish to say good night, but Bush jumped all over me at that exact instant (I think he could smell moose on me) and I had to use my hand to muzzle him so he wouldn't wake Mother and Louise.

Louise didn't say anything the next day about what time I got home. She seemed lost in her own world. That in itself was very strange, and I should have paid attention.

CHAPTER FOURTEEN

Smart: lively, alert, active, vigorous

There was a big bingo game over in St. Albert's the following Saturday and the church was hiring buses to pick people up from around the bay. A crowd was going from Riverbank. Beryl wasn't shy about suggesting I bake a butterfly cake to be raffled off at the bingo. "Why, thank you, Issy," she said, "it's so good of you to offer." Yeah, I thought, like I had a choice!

Everyone was always amazed at the butterfly cakes, but they were as easy as sin. All you had to do was bake a round layer cake, cut the layers down the middle, and turn them so the round bits just touched in the middle. Then came the icing, and with a few coloured candies for the eyes and globs of icing to finish the edges and strings of licorice for the antennae, it was done in an hour and was even fun to create.

Butterfly cakes used to be Louise's specialty and I was her helper. This was the first time I did a cake all by myself. Wish came around and I had to slap his hand to keep it out of the icing bowl, but he was a help in finding a piece of heavy cardboard to put the cake on and covering it in tinfoil. He took the cake to the wharf for me, too, and put it in the lap of one of the two girls who were in charge of the raffle.

The good news was that we made fifty-two dollars off the raffle, and with just one more raffle, *hint hint,* we'd have enough for the flowers and the decorations. The graduation committee decided that this time the cake should be a princess.

The fabric had come for the dresses and Molly organized a sewing bee. Saturday was set as the day we'd get together to fit patterns, cut out the dresses and maybe even start sewing. We planned to go over to Molly's because she had an old-fashioned pedal sewing machine, and another girl was going to bring her mother's portable Singer.

I did the princess cake right after school on Friday. I made a plain white cake in an angel food cake pan, the one with the hole in the centre. When it cooled, I carved the edge slightly with a sharp knife so it would look like a big skirt. I tucked the pieces I cut off around the little plastic carnival doll I put in the hole. Once the whole thing was iced, it looked as if the doll was wearing a big puffy pink skirt, and with the little white flowers I made with royal icing covering the dress, she did indeed look like a princess.

Louise was going over to the Legion, so she took the cake and dropped it off at the church hall.

I was just about to fall exhausted into bed, because after the cake I had to do homework, when the phone rang. Now, I still hated that darn thing. I let it ring four, five, six times while I stared at it, unable to move. Then I remembered Mother; I didn't want to wake her. I picked it up on the eighth ring.

Someone on the other end was crying. "Hello, Issy. It's me, Molly. Look, I know the girls are supposed to come to my place tomorrow, but …" And that's when she broke down and really cried.

"What's wrong, Molly? Are you okay?"

A few more sniffles. "Yes, I'm fine. It's Dad. He's not … he's sick, and I don't think I can have the girls here tomorrow." In the background I heard a man's voice shouting at Molly and telling her to get off the phone. There was so much cursing that my ears burned.

Molly's dad was a drinker, and when he got drunk he got mean. I'd heard he could go on a binge lasting two or three days, and when that happened Molly and her mother and six brothers and sisters sometimes had to take refuge at a neighbour's house.

There was a long pause, because I didn't know what I was supposed to say. Finally, I said into the plastic mouthpiece, "We can set up here, Molly. We've got a big living room and it won't be any trouble to get us organized here."

Oh goodness, did I really say that? So far I'd been able to keep a low profile at all the meetings and goings-on over the graduation. I still wasn't even certain I would pass or that I was staying for the graduation. Then I went over in my head what I'd done to date: I was the treasurer, I'd come up with the idea for the dresses and the shoes, I'd helped pick out the flowers, I'd baked two cakes for the raffle, and now here I was about to host a gaggle of girls for a sewing bee. When had I become this girl they all expected so much from?

The crying stopped. "That's wonderful, Issy. I knew I could depend on you. I've got three different kinds of squares made and

I'll bring them over, so all you have to worry about is the tea. Beryl is bringing a dozen Cokes," she said with such relief in her voice that I couldn't believe I had waited a full thirty seconds before inviting the girls over.

I had a talk with Mother the next morning. A real talk. She didn't berate me and I didn't get upset. I told her the girls were coming and that we promised to be quiet and that I would bring her a tray of tea and a small fudge square at four o'clock, her usual time. She said without any trace of a fuss, "That would be lovely, Isabelle," and went back to her TV show.

The girls showed up promptly at two o'clock. Brenda Joe and Diane Smith had the money from the raffle and were bursting with excitement. "Fifty-five dollars this time!" they squealed together.

When Louise heard the noise and learned what was going to happen, she remembered she had some paperwork to do up at the school.

We had to make copies of the pattern onto tissue paper and then we had to decide on necklines and sleeves with the intent of making each dress just a little different. I stayed quiet because I didn't know enough to know what neckline would suit me. The last time I'd worn a dress was at my great-aunt's funeral. I had but two in my closet, both ordered from the catalogue by Louise because she insisted I had to have something to wear for good.

"The square neck with the wide straps and no sleeves would be perfect for Issy," Beryl was saying. The girls stopped what they were doing.

"Yes," said Brenda, "she'll be beautiful in that." Did they see me in the room or not? Beautiful? Me? Not likely!

Wish walked into the kitchen just then, saw all the girls, went beet red and turned to leave. I had no idea there was a situation he couldn't handle.

"Didn't you tell your boyfriend you were having a hen party?" Diane asked with a giggle. I thought the question must have been for Beryl, but Diane was staring straight at me. I didn't know where to look—I saw a stray piece of cotton that needed to be picked up from the rug.

"Oh, don't go, Wish my boy," said Brenda as she stretched her neck to look out the window. "That's my mother down at the wharf, she went shopping in St. Albert's, and I asked her to see if Aunt Bernie would lend me her sewing machine. Could you go down to the landing, my love, and see if she has it? If she does, could you bring it up to us?"

I was still rooted to the same spot I was standing in when Wish walked in the door. Surely Diane was teasing me. Oh my God, I thought, Beryl is going to have a kitten! But I looked across at her and she was busy spreading out the fabric and pattern across the floor, and hardly paid Wish any attention at all.

Wish made a quick getaway and that's when Diane let out a shrill scream. What now? I thought. This was supposed to be fun.

"There's not enough fabric," she said. "See, if you lay out the pattern the way they tell you in the sewing guide, there's no way we're going to get eight dresses out of this."

We looked at the tissue pattern pieces and the copies we'd made scattered over the ribbon of fabric, and it was obvious that someone was going to have to do without a back or a front.

Mother walked into the room. "I think I heard that you need

some help," she said, not noticing the gasps or the bug eyes. I was just as surprised as everyone else but decided it was best to act like it was normal for my mother to give a helping hand when needed.

Mother had now lost about fifty pounds. This was all the weight she needed to lose according to the doctor, who had hinted that losing the weight would make her feel better about herself along with helping her heart. She was wearing a real dress, not one of her regular flowery housecoats. She had taken out the rollers she usually wore all day long, and had combed her hair into soft curls around her face. She looked like an average, everyday mom, one you could tell must have been very pretty when she was younger and who wasn't so bad-looking even now. She was as smart as anyone.

After everyone snapped their mouths shut, they made room for Mother on the chesterfield and watched her while she took a few minutes to check how we had laid out the pattern pieces. She moved a piece here and another at the end, and another two got turned upside down, and right before our eyes the puzzle pieces fit with maybe a quarter of a yard to spare.

"If you want," she said, "I can do all your measurements again and check the sizes. You don't want to make a mistake at the cutting stage. Everything else can be fixed, but once a pattern is cut you can't make it bigger."

The girls happily got in line to be measured and there were more than a few adjustments.

Meanwhile, Wish came back carrying a portable sewing machine. Mother barely looked up, but said, pretty much like a normal mom, "Issy, take this young man to my room and get him to bring out my portable machine too. It's at the bottom of my closet."

Wish was the first person outside the family to enter my mother's room since I could remember (apart from the doctor, of course). We found the sewing machine right where Mother said it would be. It wasn't my imagination that when we both reached for it, Wish kept his hand on mine for a few seconds longer than he had to by rights. I was bright pink when we came back to the living room.

"Say, what was going on back there?" Molly teased. I escaped to the kitchen to put on the kettle while Wish stayed in the living room a few minutes longer to set up the machines for Mother.

"Give the boy some tea and some of those squares," said Mother. "He's worked hard this afternoon."

Wish said he really had to get going, but with such charm that no one felt he was dying to escape.

The girls were all over Mother and she was telling them funny stories about the war and how she had to learn to sew because so many people had nothing when they were bombed out of their homes. She said she had made dozens of shirts and blouses and pairs of pyjamas for the Red Cross. She took the quarter yard of material and showed us how to make knickers and a bra with a couple of twists of the material.

None of the girls in the room was a ninny. They could all sew a little, and with Mother guiding us and making sure we did the notches so the pieces would match up in the right places and adjusting the darts and keeping the machines threaded and putting in all the zippers, the dresses and the linings were at the hanging stage by six o'clock, when the girls reluctantly went home for supper. We would finish the dresses next Saturday.

At the door there were low whispers. "Issy, your mom is some nice."

I happily made Mother a cup of tea and gave her two small walnut fudge squares as a bonus and a thank you. She ate one very slowly and gave me the other one back. "I have to be careful, you know," she said.

Louise couldn't believe her eyes when she came in. She made a fuss over the dresses, but all the time she was looking at Mother contently sitting at the kitchen table like a regular mom.

"Why don't you go rest while I get supper ready," she suggested to Mother with what sounded like awe in her voice.

"Yes, I am tired. They're lovely girls, Isabelle," she said as she went down the hall. "You have very nice friends."

Ordinary, everyday words from my mother. I went to sleep that night wondering if she was on the mend and if, just perhaps, maybe, she could one day take care of herself. Then I told myself that miracles don't happen overnight and she could still have one of her attacks at any time, and then we would all be right back at the beginning again.

SEWING THE DRESSES and planning the decorations for the tiny hall under the church was exciting, but as I gained confidence, the idea of getting a job was even more on my mind. While I used to see Mother as an anchor around my neck, holding me down, as she began to get well I understood that my wanting to get away wasn't only about her; it was also about closing the door on the me that was a failure.

At the same time, I was working hard at school and began thinking that if I passed, maybe I should stay in school. Grades ten and eleven were going to be hard too; it would take me a while to catch up on the foundation years I'd missed. But I felt for the first time that I could do it.

I'd been listening some more to the girls when they talked about their sisters up in Halifax and Toronto, the ones who hadn't graduated high school. Molly had two older sisters who left school after grade ten, and both were working in hair salons after doing courses at a beauty school. Brenda's sister was working on an assembly line in a box factory, and Diane had a sister working as a receptionist in a plant that made car parts. None of those jobs seemed as interesting to me now as they had a few months ago.

I thought of Wish, who wanted to stay in Riverbank despite his fancy schools; and I thought of Louise, who stayed, had a good job and was respected. I even thought of Lady, who chose to come back to Riverbank after seeing London and Paris and going to parties in beautiful homes. She came back because she was needed by her family. But no one forced her, it was her decision.

Whenever I could, I found a few minutes to go to Lady's grave, and I used that time to set out the pros and cons of leaving school or staying. I knew how to think things through, to weigh the advantages and disadvantages. The big barriers against staying were Mother and my own instincts. Yet Mother was changing, she was getting a little better as each week went by. As for me, I kept reminding myself that it was only a few months ago that I'd

wanted nothing more than to get a job and get away. I didn't trust
myself anymore. How could I change my mind so easily?

On the one hand, I now wanted to continue in school with my
classmates. They were a year younger than me, but I'd missed so
much growing up that it hardly mattered. On the other hand, if I
quit school and went away, I could work and get a place of my own
and start over. I could shake off my past, leave it behind like a
butterfly sheds its cocoon.

And then there was Louise. Something was happening with her
too; I couldn't help but notice. She was getting restless. It used to be
that she could sit at the kitchen table and mark papers or do report
cards for hours at a time. Now she'd work for half an hour and then
she'd jump up and pace around the kitchen and living room, make
herself a cup of coffee, and sneak out and have a cigarette. She didn't
know that I knew she had taken up smoking, but she shared a room
with me and I could smell the Player's tobacco on her clothes. She
used to spend the weekends cleaning the house and reading her
thick books, but now that she had the car she'd often be gone by ten
on Saturday morning, after a quick cleaning, and would sometimes
stay overnight in St. Albert's with her friend Maisy. Up until this
spring I couldn't remember a single night that Louise wasn't home.

She did something one Sunday that was totally unlike anything
she had ever done in my lifetime. Paul Fletcher came to the house.
He was off-duty and wanted to do some spring fishing in one of
the ponds on the barrens, but he needed a guide; it was easy to get
lost on the barrens. It was hard to turn down a chance for a walk
on a beautiful day, but after spending the Saturday doing the
dresses I had to finish my homework.

"I'll take you up," said Louise, as bold as brass. "It's been years since I was up on the barrens, but have no fear, I know my way around." She started to pack sandwiches and gather warm clothes. "Issy, find Dad's small rod for me, will you?" she asked in such a civil tongue that I got it for her without any sassing.

Our glasses had come in the mail and somehow she'd softened her hair, and without a frown on her face she was beginning to look like a woman who could be tender and gentle, given half a chance.

Louise came back that evening with a sadness about her that made me wonder if something had happened between her and Paul up on the barrens. Secretly I had been rooting for Paul, even though a marriage between the two of them would close a lock on the trap that might keep me here, since he lived in St. Albert's—just far enough away that Louise couldn't care for Mother. He was a good, decent man, and lately I'd come around to believing that Louise deserved something better than being a handmaid to Mother.

I thought maybe there was a way things could work out for both of us. Maybe I didn't have to run away, maybe I could put on my white dress and go to the graduation after all. On the other hand, maybe I'd better abandon ship while I still could.

ALL THAT THINKING took time. One morning I woke up and the trees were in bud, the breeze had a touch of warmth to it, and the paths along the river were no longer muddy from the winter runoff but dry underfoot. A tombstone appeared in the cemetery at the head of Wish's granddad's grave, a pretty one with a carving of a soldier on it, come all the way from Toronto.

Wish dropped by to ask me to bid him luck as he started off on his first day of work on the roads and promised me a picnic up the river when he got his first paycheque. He had his own little boat now, to get him across the river to his car, and he'd built a landing stage on the beach outside his granddad's house. He'd given the house a coat of dark green paint and done the doors and shutters in red, and he was very proud of how he'd rewired the whole house himself, too. He'd come by a few evenings to play with Bush—at least that's what he said—but he was mostly busy on the house, and I was busy getting ready for exams and trying to make a decision about my life.

Exam morning snuck up on me, and it seemed that in the blink of an eye I was sitting there with my classmates struggling over math problems, latitudes in geography, prime ministers in history and sentence structure in English. Miss Simms and I had talked about the exams, and she told me a dozen times if she told me once that I was to do what I could do and not to fuss about the rest. I was slow at reading and slow at putting my thoughts down in sentences that required a subject, verb and object. I had to check every sentence. I didn't make it to the end of a single exam.

I won't keep you in suspense—I passed. Yahoo! I got a 54 percent average and the whole class cheered for me.

Mother, of course, said I could do better. But Louise was so happy for me that she danced around the kitchen and clapped her hands with pure joy.

Later that night, after Mother was fast asleep, I made a pan of chocolate fudge and licked the spoon and scraped the pan while Louise drank a cup of coffee and told me what happened between her and Paul up on the barrens two weeks earlier. At first I had to pull it out of her, almost a word at a time, but when she saw I wasn't going to laugh at her, that I felt her pain, she finally opened up.

"Been up to the barrens lately?" I asked.

"No."

"Was it warm up there the day you went with the sergeant?"

"Yes."

"Did he catch any fish?" I asked, doing some fishing myself.

"Yes."

"He didn't come in to fry them up," I noted, not a question but an observation that left things hanging.

Louise didn't say anything but turned away from me and looked out the window.

"He's a nice man," I said, and got up to put water in the fudge pan and set it in the sink to soak. Then I said, as if it had just crossed my mind, "You know, Louise, I think he'll make some woman a wonderful husband." I sat down then and looked at her and saw two big, fat tears swimming in her eyes.

"He has no intention of ever being a husband to anyone," she said, dropping her face into her folded arm on the table.

I waited. That was one thing I was good at. I never felt the need to fill silences.

"He says he can't marry because the job is so dangerous and he won't leave a woman waiting at home wondering if he's dead or alive." She sniffled and carried on.

"He had a partner out in British Columbia who was shot and killed when they stopped a driver for speeding on the highway.

Paul had to go and tell the wife, and he says he'll never forget her anguish."

"But I could have sworn he had a serious crush on you."

"Yes, he told me as much. But he said he had to find the strength to fight the attraction. He said he was going to ask for a transfer."

I could tell from Louise's body-racking sobs that while her pride had been hurt when Dr. David dropped her, her heart was breaking over Paul.

We sat together in the kitchen for a long time. I let her cry until there were no more tears, and then I turned out the lights and told her she needed her sleep because, despite everything, we still had to get on with our lives.

MY NEXT DILEMMA was whether to stay for the graduation. My lovely dress with the square neck and wide straps that fit like a soft glove was hanging in my closet; my shoes, an old pair of Louise's, were ready with two coats of milky white; the flowers and decorations were paid for. Our graduation was planned for two days after school closed. The teachers were doing a graduation for the kindergarten class going into grade one; and, with all the fuss about our grad, the grade six class wanted one too, for graduating into junior high. Being a thrifty school, we were using the same decorations for all three.

School closed for the summer on June 18, the grad was planned for the 20th, a Friday, and my birthday was Saturday, June 21. Somehow I was still hanging around on the 18th. My feet felt like concrete slabs every time I thought of packing a little bag and slipping away. I knew all about the old expression "He who hesitates is lost"—and I was beginning to feel quite lost. Eventually I had to admit to myself that I was getting excited about the graduation and that I was looking forward to the picnic with Wish, which was going to be on our birthday. I finally decided I would stay, at least for the graduation and my birthday.

It seemed I dilly-dallied too long. The night of the 18th, Louise went missing.

CHAPTER FIFTEEN

*Killick: an anchor made up of an elongated stone encased
in pliable sticks bound at the top and fixed in two curved
crosspieces, used in mooring nets and small boats*

I was waiting for Louise up at St. Ann's after school because
she'd asked me to help her carry home some of the stuff from
her desk on the last day of school. I didn't mind giving her a hand
now that she asked with a civil tongue in her head.

Then Miss Simms told me she had seen Louise leave the school.
That was odd, because I hadn't seen her go down the road to our
place, and she had told me to wait—she was very definite about
that. I went home and discovered Mother in the kitchen making tea.
This in itself was astounding, but I don't think I really took it in.

"Mother," I said rather bluntly, "have you seen Louise?"

"Not at all, and it's way past my tea time. She's always here for
my tea," said Mother, but I brushed past her to go to the bedroom
to see if perhaps Louise was lying down with a headache.

Not a sign of her. It was only three-thirty on a beautiful June
day and I convinced myself she would be home shortly. I went

back to the kitchen to see to Mother and to look out the window. I couldn't tell if Louise's car was across the river or not; it was easily hidden by the trees now that they were in full leaf.

"What do you want for supper?" Mother asked shortly after watching *General Hospital*. Now that threw me for a loop. I didn't think Mother knew how to turn on the stove. She was searching through the cupboards. "What about boiled eggs?"

I had to smile. It wasn't a gourmet meal, but if that's what she wanted to cook for supper, it was fine with me.

"We'll eat while watching *The Mary Tyler Moore Show*," I suggested. I was restless and, yes, getting a little worried.

Mother went to her room after the show and left me to tidy up the kitchen. One step at a time, I thought as I cleaned up burnt toast and water that had overflowed and scorched the stovetop.

Nine o'clock and still no Louise. I didn't know who to call or what to do. I certainly didn't want to alarm Mother or give her a shock. I was heartsick, knowing it would be unbearable if anything happened to my sister.

At ten o'clock I had no option but to make some calls. I still hated the phone, but at least now I could see the numbers in the phone book and on the dial. I called Miss Simms first. No, she hadn't seen Louise and suggested I call Louise's friend Maisy over in St. Albert's. No, she hadn't seen Louise either, but maybe she was at the Legion? I knew that wasn't possible and decided not to embarrass myself or Louise by calling there. Out of desperation, I phoned Wish. Yes, he had seen her—driving up the road to Grand Falls like a bat out of hell around two o'clock, exactly when I was waiting for her up at the school.

"What's wrong, Issy? You sound like you're trying to stay calm, but it's not working, I know you too well."

"Louise didn't tell anyone she was leaving to go anywhere. I don't know where she is."

"I'll be right over," Wish said, and he was true to his word, quietly coming into the kitchen five minutes later, slightly out of breath.

While I was waiting for him, I had gone through some of Louise's things. I wasn't certain, but it looked like some of her better clothes were missing. I told Wish this.

"I think you're going to have to call the police, Issy. Ask for Sergeant Fletcher."

The sergeant was on duty and I recognized his voice right away.

"It's Issy Heffernan, Sergeant. Look, my sister hasn't come home this evening. It's very unlike her. She's never not come home in her life. My friend Wish says he saw her driving up the highway to Grand Falls at two o'clock this afternoon. It's close to midnight. She hasn't phoned. I'm very worried."

There was a long silence. "Is your friend there? Put him on the line," said Sergeant Fletcher in a tone that brooked no argument.

"Yes, sir, it was definitely her. I know her car ... No, she didn't see me ... She was wearing a white blouse ... She was driving pretty fast ... We'll wait here by the phone in case she calls."

That's when I started to cry. I couldn't believe that something might have happened to Louise. For all the hard years we had been through together, I knew then that I loved her and that I would miss her terribly if ... if anything happened to her. Wish led me gently to the chesterfield and sat with his arm around me. He didn't say silly things like "Everything will be okay" or "I bet she's got a flat tire," because he knew I only wanted hard information. I was dreading having to get Mother up.

To help me take my mind off Louise and all the ugly possibilities, he told me the story of the Heffernans and the Sweetapples.

"Great-aunt Effie told me about it after Grandfather's funeral. She said he made her vow never to talk about it while he was alive. The nut of it was that Lady and my grandfather were betrothed when he went away to the war in 1916," he started, and that got me to sit up straight.

"She hated waiting, so Lady joined up too and, as you know, went to Britain and was a secretary in the War Office. He was in the trenches in France. He never got her letters and he didn't know she was in London. Six months after she arrived, they coincidentally went to the same officers' dance—she with her boss and he with a nurse from his battalion. Of course, they each thought the worst. She broke off the engagement that night and he was just as happy that she did. Effie said she was the one who discovered the misunderstanding.

"Lady stayed in London, but then your grandmother died and Lady was asked to come home to raise your dad. A year earlier my grandfather had married my grandmother. Effie tried to tell him it was a misunderstanding, but he wouldn't listen to his sister and always believed that Lady had wronged him. Great-aunt Effie said Lady was trained to do high-level office work and would have done quite well in Grand Falls or St. John's, but she stayed in Riverbank to help the family, and maybe, Great-aunt Effie said, to be close to Granddad," he finished off.

I knew what that had cost her. She had so little when she died—the house and furniture she grew up with, and the things she'd made so her home would look bright and cozy. From the photo I saw at Great-aunt Effie's, I knew there was a time when she was an admired young woman who got invited to parties in beautiful homes.

"You and I might have been cousins," I said.

"Ah, then maybe it was all for the best."

I wasn't quite sure what he meant, and we both went deep into our own thoughts.

I must have fallen asleep. The next thing I knew, Wish was shaking me awake. The porch door was opening and Bush wasn't making a racket. I checked the clock—it was two a.m.

Louise walked in carrying a small suitcase, and behind her was Sergeant Fletcher with a bigger suitcase. I recognized the set because they belonged to Mother.

"I won't stay," said the sergeant, "it's late. I'll call in the morning." And right there in front of me and Wish, Louise reached up on tiptoe and kissed him on the mouth. Well!

"Go to bed, Issy," she said. "I promise to tell you all about it tomorrow."

I didn't mind being bossed around, to be honest. I was just so happy she was home safe and sound.

LOUISE'S STORY is almost unbelievable, but if she says it happened, then it happened, because Louise has never told a lie or a tall tale in her life.

She had decided to run away. All this time I was planning my own escape, she was plotting hers. I didn't tell her about me, of course, though it was hard to keep from smiling at the fact that she had got one over on me and didn't know it.

She said that she decided Mother could probably manage on her own if she had to, that I would be going across the harbour to high school and that if she didn't make a break for it she'd never get away. She said a few times that she never thought I would have to stay with Mother. She said she would never have left if that were the case. (She was kinder to me than I planned to be to her.)

And her plans were a lot more ambitious than mine. She said that all her life Mother had told her stories about England and that her own memories were vague but pleasant. She was determined to go back and visit the places she already knew so much about. Louise was booked on the five p.m. flight to Shannon and London out of Gander International Airport. So you see, she told me, she had to leave at two to get there on time; any later than that and she wouldn't have made it. "Even then, I had to drive a lot faster than I liked.

"I couldn't tell you, because you might have told Mother. The two of you have been quite cozy lately, and I didn't want to face Mother's histrionics. That was the whole point of leaving without saying goodbye. I was going to phone from Gander before you had time to worry about me.

"About an hour from the airport, there was a freak snowstorm. Now I've seen snow in June in Newfoundland, and even July, but when I left Riverbank it was a lovely sunny day, so I wasn't expecting a snowstorm. I had to slow down and I was really concerned I wouldn't make it. But I did. I pulled into the parking lot twenty minutes before flight time. There was no time to phone home, just to slosh through the snow in my summer sandals. I was the last person to check in. My heart was pounding in my chest, but I'd made it.

"Everyone else was already on the plane. I was barely in my seat when the door was shut and I knew 'This is it, I'm going to England, no more doubts.' Five o'clock came and went, and the stewardesses were filling time, handing out pillows and orange juice. At 5:45 the captain said that we'd be delayed at least another half-hour because of the storm. He said they had to plough the runway.

"At seven o'clock, we're still sitting on the tarmac and I'm wondering if I'm actually going to get away after all. I was even starting to wonder if I was doing the right thing. The longer I sat in the plane, the more the excitement wore off. I was beginning to feel foolish—me, a thirty-four-year-old school principal, running away from my mother.

"Then the pilot came on and said we were going. That's it, I told myself, the decision is made. We lumbered to the end of the runway, the engines revved, the plane shook, and then … nothing. The pilot came on the intercom and said we had 'missed our window of opportunity' and the runway had to be ploughed again. We turned back. It was now eight o'clock.

"I grabbed the hand of one of the stewardesses and said to her, 'I don't think I should be on this plane. I'm needed at home. My mother …' And I couldn't say anything else, I was so choked up. You know, it was like she heard this kind of thing all the time. 'You're the reason we're not taking off,' she said. 'You need to be with your mother. I'll speak to the captain.' She came back five minutes later and said it was no trouble to open the door and find my bag because they were going to be on the tarmac for a while yet anyway.

"I got to my car and found it was covered in six inches of snow. I laughed out loud, I was so giddy. I wanted to get home as fast as I could so no one would miss me. I was glad I hadn't phoned before we took off. I'm so thankful you didn't tell Mother, Issy. I owe you for that."

"It had to be more than Mother," I said, thinking that surely she'd noticed that Mother was getting better.

"Yes, you're right. When Dr. David chose Shirley Cameron over me, it opened my eyes to the fact that no prince charming was going to swoop in and change my life for me. I've wanted to leave for years but could never get up the nerve. After Shirley, I knew for certain that if I wanted to change my life, I had to do it myself.

"And then Paul told me that he never wanted to get married, no matter what he felt. I knew then I had better make my own lemon-ade out of life's bitter lemons."

"So what happened next?"

"It took me two hours to drive from Gander to Grand Falls because of the slippery roads, and by this time it was after ten o'clock. I dreaded the idea of going down our road by myself and at that time of the night. The snow had stopped, so I wasn't concerned about that anymore, just the darkness and knowing there wasn't another human being until I got down to our end of the road, a full two hours away.

"A half-hour down the road I got a flat tire. About ten minutes later, I saw headlights coming toward me and I wondered who would be out at this hour of the night. It was a police cruiser going about eighty miles an hour. The car was just a blur as it passed and I thought something bad must have happened somewhere down the coast. Then, the brakes squealed and the car turned around. Next thing, the cruiser pulls up beside me and the police officer is pointing at me, telling me to get in his car.

"It was only then that I realized it was Paul. He was pretty mad but not about my flat tire.

"'Where in the hell were you tonight?' he asked as I opened the passenger door. He calmed down a bit when he saw I was okay and told me that you had called and were worried sick about me. I won't bore you with all the details, but I gave him heck for scaring the life out of me with his flashing light. We ended up having a long talk there in the middle of the highway. He said that thinking something might have happened to me had made him realize that life is full of complications, and he wanted to share whatever was ahead with me.

"And that's where he asked me to marry him. Honest to goodness, there wasn't another human being for miles and it was as silent as the grave. The only light was from his flashers that he forgot to turn off. So romantic!"

"So you told him yes," I said.

"Oh no, in my day a girl didn't let a guy think she was easy. I told him he was to come to supper tonight and I'd tell him yes then," she said with a grin that grew into a laugh. "Tonight you act real good at the table and then disappear, okay? And don't you tell a soul this story," she commanded. "I have to keep up my reputation, you know."

I told her that of course she could trust me not to tell a soul. And I didn't.

THEN DAD CAME HOME. Not just for a visit, but for good. It was amazingly easy for him in the end. It seems he heard me say "buy a boat" when I thought I'd said it under my breath. And that's exactly what he came home to do.

He didn't just up and leave his job with the CN boats; my father was a careful man. He told us the power plant had been after him for years to come home and be a manager, and he'd refused because he didn't particularly want to come home to an office job on the land, and he wasn't all that keen to be at home, period. Neither of those reasons was a secret to Louise or me. Since his last trip, he'd done a lot of research and a number of letters had gone back and forth. He accepted an offer from the power plant to be the vice-president of operations, and in the middle of July he was going to Nova Scotia to pick up the small yacht he'd designed and was having built there.

"Can't wait to be captain," he said, pulling out some coastal charts. "I'm going to sail her back here and I've figured out a way I can sail her over to the plant during the summer. I'll have to buy a car for the winter, but I'm going to keep the *Agnes H.* in the water as long as I can."

I'd like to say that Dad made it home in time for the graduation and that he smiled at me as I walked down the little aisle in the church basement with my diploma under my arm. But I can't tell a lie—he came home a week later. I wasn't expecting him for the graduation, though, so I didn't mind. Louise was there as the prin-

cipal, of course. But it was Mildred and her six brothers and
sisters, all spruced up in pressed pants and ironed blouses and
shirts, who beamed at me all through the little ceremony.

Mother wasn't at the school either. She said she came to the
window and watched the flicker of our candles in the thick night.
It was enough, because I understood what a big effort it took for
her to get even that close to the outside world. She loaned me a
pearl bracelet she said had been given to her when she was a girl,
and she hosted a little party, with the whole class coming to our
house for a midnight mug-up.

Louise did most of the cooking, but Mother was there, dressed
in a new pantsuit and very excited about seeing the girls wearing
their dresses. Diane Smith was getting a tour of Mother's charm
bracelet when her high heel gave out. She grabbed the kitchen
tablecloth and pulled so hard that two of Mother's precious
Belleek teacups shattered into dozens of little pieces. I froze and
Louise sputtered, but Mother simply waved her hand over the
mess as if to say "Not to worry." She told the girls that when she
was feeling a little better she was going to take me with her on a
trip back to England.

"That china pattern is easy to replace, it never gets discontin-
ued. I may even get myself a new set of china while I'm there, I'm
getting tired of that one," she quipped as she turned toward the
kitchen.

At two o'clock in the morning, she sent me out to the shed for
her old evening dresses. Louise had put them away very carefully
in two cedar trunks, using layers of tissue paper. All the girls were
green with envy as I tried on one of the nicest. It fit me perfectly.

So YES, in the end, I put on the white dress and shoes and pinned
on the red roses and joined my classmates for the graduation.
After I recovered from Louise's story and after I saw her engagement ring, it was too late to back out. Everyone was expecting me
there. And I kind of wanted to go anyway.

The ceremony was very pretty because of the candles and the
darkness, and with us all dressed in white we looked like fairies
drifting through the warm, thick forest toward the music in the
church. The boys looked sharp too, in grey flannels and navy
blazers with little red rosebuds in their lapels. Oh yes, and we
borrowed Sergeant Fletcher and asked him to wear his red serge
and march at the beginning of our little procession. He tried to
explain that there were definite rules about when he was allowed
to wear his formal dress uniform, but I had Louise ask him
again and finally he said he wouldn't wear the full uniform but
enough to get the point across. Beryl gave a little talk and
thanked me in front of everyone for being a real trooper for
helping out so much. I blushed so deeply my face matched the
roses on my dress.

I wore Great-aunt Lady's cross for the last time that night.
When all the girls had gone home and Mother was in bed, I took
it off and gave it to Louise. "I want you to wear this at your
wedding," I said. "It'll be something old."

"Why, Issy, that's the nicest thing that anyone has ever done for
me. I'll keep it safe for you," said Louise.

"No. Yes, I mean, keep it safe. But I want you to have it. I think
Dad made a mistake in giving it to me. You'll know how to take
care of it properly," I mumbled as I tried to find the words to make

her understand that I thought Lady had loved her just as much as she loved me.

"Thank you," said Louise with a crack in her voice, "I know the cross means a lot to you and I'll always remember this." And then she hugged me, a real tight sisterly hug.

Wish told me I was the prettiest girl at the graduation, but I imagine every girl heard that from someone before the evening was finished.

Beryl probably heard it from her boyfriend. Yes, that's what I said, her *boyfriend*. All through the winter and spring, Beryl had been "dating" an older boy from Head of the Bay, a town close to the hydro plant. He was twenty and in the army, posted to training camps in Nova Scotia and Ontario. She wrote him a letter every night and he promised all along to come home for her graduation. Apparently everyone knew this except me and her parents. None so blind as those who will not see.

Wish and I got to our birthday picnic, but not alone. Word went around during the coffee and sandwiches at the graduation about what we were planning, and in the blink of an eye six couples were coming with us the next day. Wish and I rowed there in his small boat and he moored it with the old-fashioned killick anchor he'd made by using sketches he found in his grandfather's desk. We had a lunch at high noon under the eagles' nest up near the clay banks. Wish gave me a scarf in shades of gold and brown that the girls said was exactly the right colour for me. "Cashmere," said Wish for my ears only. "And it's not for drying off Bush." As I tried it on, a little blue box fell out, and inside was a silver charm for my bracelet, a heart with *Wish* written on the back. Again he whispered into my ear: "It's both of our initials, see, intertwined." And I did see, and I felt my mouth tremble up with the wonder of it.

I gave him a six-inch camel hair paintbrush for his birthday. That's what he said he wanted when I asked him.

So you see, I was too busy to leave and it was just so much easier to go with the flow. Dad was coming home, Louise was getting married, and she and Paul were fixing up Lady's house and moving in there to keep an eye on Mother, and Mother wanted to sew Louise's dress and mine, and I was to help her. I was to be the maid of honour.

It was likely that Louise and Paul would live in Lady's house for a while, because Paul was still new to our area and wouldn't be asked to transfer for another two years at least. Louise blushed when she told me that she would help Mother get back on her feet as long as she could—until the babies started coming.

"Later, Paul will ask for a transfer to St. John's so I can get my master's degree."

Wish was saying he might quit his road job because my father wanted him to go to Nova Scotia with him to help sail the boat back. Wish had done some sailing on the Great Lakes and was keen to get experience on the open seas. He admitted that hard labour on the roads wasn't quite as romantic as it seemed at the beginning. He was talking about boarding up the house for the winter but coming back again next April after university, and Dad was saying there'd be a summer job for him at the power plant, especially if he was interested in engineering work. Wish did have a knack for fixing things, and he said rewiring his granddad's house was the most interesting work he had ever done. He said that an engineer could help out in poor countries, and that appealed to him too.

"You wouldn't mind going to Africa for a couple of years, would you? You'd be great with the little ones," he said to me one evening soon after Louise's engagement.

Me? Africa?! Me, with Wish, all those years down the road! I searched his face to see if he knew what he was asking, and his slow smile told me that he did. I felt a warmth creeping up my neck, but for once I didn't hide my thoughts. I smiled back at Wish and he knew my answer. No words had passed between us; instead, he took my hand and sealed our bargain with a gentle squeeze.

I WAS WORKING on getting myself invited on the boat trip from Nova Scotia so we could have more time together. I was planning to start my driving lessons soon, though when Sergeant Fletcher— I mean Paul—took me for a little test drive, he appeared a bit nervous. He said my perception seemed to be off, and that I was to give myself lots of room and to park way back from ditches and embankments.

I got in a real flap about where I would board in September in St. Albert's. Everyone else had set up their boarding houses in January and February, when Miss Simms handed out the forms. Then one night the phone rang and Louise handed it to me. It was Wish's great-aunt Effie, who told me she would love to have me as a boarder. I remembered that she lived close to the school and that she used to be a teacher. "Yes," I said right away, "that would be perfect."

I don't know why, but maybe because Dad was talking about the letters he had written to the power plant about his job and Beryl was writing this mysterious boyfriend of hers, I suddenly remembered where I'd stashed the letters Wish had written me when I was twelve and he was fifteen. There were two, and I hadn't opened either—I knew it was useless back then. There had been other letters when he first went away, but I burned all of those in fits of frustration. These two came later, out of the blue, and I hid them in my bottom drawer because it was summer and there was no fire in the wood stove.

One night when Louise was out with Paul, making wedding plans, I read both letters. The first was reminding me that no matter what happened, he would be there for me. The second, written a couple of weeks later, said he couldn't understand why I'd not written him back, but that he forgave me anyway. He went on to tell me about his new school and his first school dance. "None of the girls is as pretty as you, Issy. I told them I had a girl-friend already. I hope you don't mind me saying that about you, because it's the way I feel. You and I are meant to be together. I hope you can tell me that you feel the same way about me. I'll come back as soon as I can. Love, your Wish."

I held the letter to my heart, closed my eyes and remembered Wish's first kiss from the night before. He had waited long and patiently for his answer.

A Note from the Author

Most authors plan a series. This one happened by chance, quite late one night when I was writing this book and a character from my first book, *Seven for a Secret*, boldly marched onto the page. It was then, finally, that I accepted I needed to write the continuing stories of my Cook's Cove families.

I realized I still had many stories to tell, based on my own growing-up years in Newfoundland, especially stories about girls finding their place in a very real world and whose main connections are with the wind-blown land, the turbulent sea and a history of struggle. I work to create homes and families that reflect the social history of our outports using the humour that is our strength.

In all there will be seven books in the series, one for each line of the nursery rhyme that appears at the beginning of *One for Sorrow* (though not necessarily in that order). The next book in the series will be *Three for a Wedding*.

—Mary C. Sheppard

Acknowledgments

A novel may come out of nothing and a writer spends a great deal of time alone while writing it. But in the end it takes a small village to get it to the bookstore and into your hands.

I wish to thank my friends Marilyn Smith and Cheryl Rowe who read early versions of this book and gave valuable guidance. Also, my mother-in-law, Florence Hickey, who died Christmas 2006 but who had read and re-read the manuscript several times. She was a voracious reader and very encouraging about this book.

I thank my daughters, Melanie and Rebecca-Anne, who were sounding boards for the inner lives of teenage girls and who lent me several of their stories.

A special thank you to my husband, Paul Hickey, who ensured I had the time to write.

To my parents, Mary and George Sheppard, who told me their stories and believed that someday I would be a writer.

And a big thank you to the two very important people who pushed me along the road to finishing and helped to shape the story: my agent, Lise Henderson, and my editor at Penguin, Barbara Berson.